MATT DICKINSON

shrine
bell

www.shrinebell.com

The Everest Files
Matt Dickinson

First published in 2014 by Vertebrate Publishing. Reprinted in 2015 and 2016.
Reprinted in 2017, 2018 and 2020 by Shrine Bell, an imprint of Vertebrate Publishing.

Shrine Bell
Omega Court, 352 Cemetery Road, Sheffield S11 8FT, UK
www.shrinebell.com

A CIP catalogue record for this book is available from the British Library.

ISBN 978-1-906148-92-8 (Paperback)
ISBN 978-1-906148-93-5 (Ebook)
ISBN 978-1-911342-99-1 (Audiobook)

10 9 8 7 6

Production by Vertebrate Publishing
www.v-publishing.co.uk

Shrine Bell and Vertebrate Publishing are committed
to printing on paper from sustainable sources.

MIX
Paper from
responsible sources
FSC® C018072

Printed and bound in Great Britain by Clays Ltd, Elcograf S.p.A.

This book is dedicated to
Lhakpa Gelu Sherpa
Mingma Dorje Sherpa
Phur Gyalzen Sherpa

Steadfast and courageous companions on my
Everest North Face ascent. Together we survived
the killer storm that cost twelve lives. The summit
photograph above shows *(L-R)* Lhakpa Gelu Sherpa,
Phur Gyalzen Sherpa and author Matt Dickinson.

CHAPTER 1

We must have been about eight hours into the flight when the captain came on the tannoy.

'Good morning ladies and gentlemen.'

I was awake anyway, much too stoked to sleep.

'For those of you who are interested, there's a remarkable view of Mount Everest on the starboard side of the aircraft. Cabin crew, ten minutes to landing.'

I flipped open the plastic window blind and drank in the view. All the other gap year volunteers sitting around me were doing the same and I wished they'd stop yelling dumb stuff like 'awesome!' and enjoy it in the silence it deserved.

Because the captain was right: Everest really was something else; bigger and more stunning than I could ever have imagined. The whole plane was alive with it – there was this sort of jet-lagged electric crackle of excitement fizzing about the cabin.

I wondered if the face I was looking at had ever been climbed, and, if so, what type of superhuman hero/nutter would have taken such a risk. It looked insanely dodgy, razor sharp ridges pumping out clouds of billowing ice crystals. Unforgiving chunks of dark rock soaring in vertical steps.

'Extreme,' muttered the girl sitting next to me.

I couldn't have put it better myself.

'Ladies and gentlemen, we are now on our final approach into Kathmandu. At this time we ask you to ensure your tray table is stowed away, your seat belt fastened and your seat in the upright position. Please note that the toilets are no longer in use.'

The engines started to lose power. I felt my stomach lurch as the aeroplane went into a sharp turn. Now we could see detail in the dark terrain beneath us; wild, forested valleys which were deep and forbidding.

There were hardly any villages. Hardly any roads.

The mood around me shifted quite a bit in that moment;

this was the type of wilderness we would all be trekking into over the next six weeks, paired up in teams of two and delivering medical supplies to remote areas of Nepal.

We'd all felt so grown up when we got on the flight back in London. But now it was all real I think we just felt like a bunch of eighteen-year-old kids who had no idea what they were getting into.

As for me, what was I expecting? An adventure? A challenge? A chance to give something back before I went off to uni to study to be a vet?

Well, all of those things, and more. I was up for anything, basically.

The aeroplane lost height. The wilderness gave way to patchwork squares of water, I guessed they must be paddy fields of rice glittering in the early morning sun. We touched down gently and walked down the steps into the humid, smog-filled air of the Kathmandu valley.

A massive wall of grey cloud had already swept across the far mountains.

There was no sign of Everest at all.

O

A 'shake-down' week followed in Kathmandu and we got into the mood of the place. A lot of those early nerves were snuffed out by the realisation of just how friendly and kind the Nepali people are.

The charity put us up in a dormitory place not far from 'Freak Street' – the city's legendary hippy zone, so we were right in the heart of the action.

They taught us how to barter for stuff in the bazaars, never accepting the first price but always haggling it down. We were warned about rabid dogs (carry a big stick), taught how to filter our drinking water, and given a crash course in the local language.

Then, a few days before we were due to start the mountain journeys, my trek partner Liam got sick. He'd been eating kebabs from street stalls so no one was very sympathetic. The head guy at the charity reckoned he'd be 'all right in twenty-four hours', but he wasn't.

In fact it turned out to be amoebic dysentery so that was Liam off the trip.

For a while it looked like my whole mission might be cancelled. There was no one to take Liam's place. But it really was urgent that the medical supplies got out to their destination and, finally, the head of the charity asked me if I was prepared to do the journey on my own.

'It's a big responsibility,' he warned.

I told him I had no problem with it. I'd grown up on a

dairy farm in Northumberland, and, since I was fifteen, my parents had left me in charge when they went on holidays. If I could cope with that, I told him, I reckoned I could cope with anything.

Secretly I was kind of pleased. It meant the whole thing was much more of an adventure.

Four days later I set off on a 6 a.m. bus ride from Kathmandu. It was an amazing feeling to finally be on the road; the world I had come from seemed a million miles away. Cramming for A levels; jamming my head with facts and figures; turning out for the first XV rugby team on wet Saturday mornings. It was all behind me now; I was heading on my own, deep into the Himalaya, to a village called Tanche that I couldn't even find on Google Earth.

It felt pretty outrageous.

Sepagat was the end of the road, a steamy shanty town which was so plastered with mud that it looked like a muck spreader had gone crazy. It had been raining for twenty-four hours and fast-moving trucks had splattered everything with filth: the people, the street dogs, the tatty goods in the roadside shacks.

A hungry-eyed group of men clustered around me.

'You need porter, my friend?'

With the amount of baggage I had, there was no way I

5

was going anywhere without some help.

'I have donkey, mister, very strong donkey.'

The scrum was getting a bit lively. So, needing to sort the situation out before things got out of hand, I picked the strongest looking man for the task.

His name was Dhorjee.

We agreed on a price of two thousand rupees to transport the supplies to Tanche. More or less twenty dollars. Dhorjee and I would each carry a rucksack. The heavy barrel of medical equipment would, he said, go by donkey.

'How many hours trekking is it to Tanche?' I asked him.

'Plenty hours,' he replied vaguely. 'Up and down, up and down!'

Dhorjee proposed a quick visit to a local bar and, not wanting to offend him, I agreed. Three beers later (I stuck to Sherpa tea), we quit the bar and put on the rucksacks ready for the trek.

'Where's the barrel?' I asked him, seeing no sign of the heaviest luggage.

'Gone ahead,' he told me. 'Donkey very fast! Very strong.'

'OK.'

We set out into the early afternoon, the trail quickly getting steep as we began the haul up the valleyside.

I soon began to overheat. After just ten minutes my T-shirt was already soaked with sweat.

'How far did you say it was?' I asked Dhorjee again.

'We will be there before night,' he replied. Then he slapped me on the back with a meaty fist. 'You have cigarette for me, my friend?'

'No.'

The lack of tobacco seemed to put Dhorjee in a bad mood and he gradually pulled ahead of me, never looking back. I soon lost sight of him and there was no sign of the promised donkey. Or my barrel. Still, I kept on up the side of this huge valley, quite enjoying the trail as it punched through the forest.

A couple of hours went past and I was surprised not to have made it to the village and even more surprised that Dhorjee seemed to have totally vanished. The path had changed in a bad way, the stones becoming treacherously slippery and sharp.

At 5.30 p.m. it began to rain. A nasty wind kicked off and, to my surprise, I found I was starting to feel chilled. The temperature had dropped a lot with the gain in altitude and a cold front had swept in.

If I'd had my extra clothes I could have done something about it but, stupidly, my personal gear was in the bag that

Dhorjee had on his back.

Where was the village? What was going on? I was beginning to wonder if I had made a big mistake with this dodgy porter.

The antibiotics alone would be worth a fortune on the black market. I could just see myself returning to Kathmandu, my tail between my legs, having blown the whole mission.

Finally, after a climb that had to have been a thousand metres or more, I reached a high col and was able to see ahead. I was pinning my hopes that Tanche would now be in view but instead there was this second vast valley, perhaps even wilder and deeper than the one I had just got across.

And still there was no sign of Dhorjee.

I was starting to get stressed, fearing that the situation was getting out of control. Briefly I thought about turning round, but it was too far to go back.

I would just have to keep going.

I started trekking again but the track quickly became a muddy mess.

Then I saw a splash of red.

Blood.

Someone ahead of me was bleeding and it was only natural for me to wonder about it.

Was it Dhorjee? If so, what had happened to him?

I started walking faster, curious to catch up with whoever it was. A short while later I saw an even bigger splash of red, as if the wounded one had rested there for a bit.

A few more switchbacks on the trail. Six or seven more bloodspots and I had the wounded one in sight; well at least I had a blurred vision of a small figure dressed in a blue cape. It looked like a kid carrying a massive load and it was obvious they were exhausted.

'Hey!' I called. 'Are you OK?' The figure stopped and I saw it was a girl, sixteen or seventeen years old at a guess. She was wearing a pair of worn-out canvas sneakers which were totally ripped and torn. She had a deep cut on her ankle and it was still bleeding.

On her back was a massive load. She was literally staggering under the weight of it and I realised with a hot flash of rage that it was *my* fifty-kilo barrel of medical supplies that this poor girl was carrying on her back.

She took off the barrel as I got closer, sitting heavily on the ground, looking completely done in. Her face was streaked with mud and sweat.

'Do you speak English?' I asked her.

'Yes.'

'Who gave you that barrel?' I demanded.

'Dhorjee.'

'And how much is he paying you?'

The girl looked at her hands and did not reply.

'It's all right,' I told her wearily, 'I'm not angry with you. I'm angry with him for giving you that load.'

I sat down next to the girl, suddenly seriously tired. I found a last muesli bar in my pack and split it in two to share. She smiled briefly as she took the snack, her face coming alive.

'My name's Ryan. What's your name?' I asked her.

'Shreeya.'

'You've hurt your foot.'

'Yes.' She stared down at her bloody ankle, shivering a bit with the cold.

'I can put a bandage on it if you like.'

'Thank you.'

I cracked open the seal on the barrel and found some disinfectant and a bandage. I'd done plenty of first aid training on the charity course so this was easy stuff. Five minutes later I had the wound nicely cleaned although I reckoned the dressing wouldn't last too long in the rain.

Then the million-dollar question.

'How far is it to Tanche?'

'A few hours.'

'A few *hours*? Then we'd better get moving. I'll take the barrel.'

I gave her my rucksack, reducing her load by fifty per cent at a stroke.

The girl had been carrying the barrel in the local way, with a leather strap around her forehead. I decided to try it and managed to get it up on my back as she had done. The weight was unbelievable. The bones in my spine felt like they were grinding to dust with every step.

The more it went on the more I cursed that idiot Dhorjee. My thoughts about him were turning ugly and getting uglier with every passing step.

I wished I hadn't paid him in advance.

The rain had cranked itself up into a deluge; it was driving down with amazing force, smashing the ground to submission. Fist-sized rocks started to tumble down the slope above us and at one dicey place the path had been swept away completely by a landslide. We crossed that one hand-in-hand, Shreeya moving sure-footedly despite the terrible state of her shoes.

When I next checked my watch it was a few minutes before 10 p.m. We shared a few dried apricots and made no effort to try and find shelter. There was no point; we couldn't get any wetter. Or colder. My teeth were chattering like mad.

Finally we saw a light flickering in the distance.

'Tanche,' Shreeya said.

Not a moment too soon.

We entered the village and I stared at the dark buildings which were clustered on either side of the trail, wondering why no one was there to greet me. My mind was so messed up I could hardly remember what they had told me back in Kathmandu.

'It's OK,' Shreeya said kindly, 'you can stay with us.'

We plodded up a series of steps cut into the hillside until we came to a sturdy timber building which was journey's end.

Inside was an elderly woman with long dark plaits.

'My aunt,' Shreeya said.

I greeted her with a 'Namaste', seeing the flash of gold teeth in the thin smile she returned. She didn't look best pleased to have an unexpected house guest.

I dumped the barrel in with the goats and chickens on the ground floor and followed my hosts up a wooden ladderway.

'You can sleep here.' Shreeya showed me to a store room. Piles of potatoes were stacked in one corner, hessian sacks of some sort in another. But there was plenty of space for me to set up my sleeping stuff and the floor was dusty rather than dirty.

'Is OK?'

'Is perfect.'

I climbed into the sleeping bag and lay there, thinking about the day. I was bone tired but a smouldering core of anger about the stunt that Dhorjee had pulled kept me awake for a while.

Mice were scratching around in the potato pile. Some kind of owl was crying outside.

Down in the kitchen I could hear Shreeya and her aunt talking. The aunt seemed to be complaining about something. Her voice went on and on, droning away at Shreeya who seemed to have little to say in return.

It was strange but I just couldn't get warm, even after I put on an extra fleece and wrapped a woollen scarf around my neck.

The last thing I remember thinking before I fell asleep was 'I hope I don't get sick'.

O

It was still dark when the dawn chorus kicked off; the air rang with cockerel cries, yapping dogs and clucking chickens. Soon I heard the clatter of pans from the kitchen and the metallic squeak of the hand pump as Shreeya drew water from the well.

I dozed until daylight then went to the yard and found a bucket of water for a wash. Getting the mud and sweat off my body was sheer heaven and I felt much better.

At that moment Shreeya came back into the yard. She was wearing a red silk kameez and carrying a brass tray which held flower petals, a bowl of water and a little saucer of cooked rice. What a contrast to her rain-soaked appearance of the previous night. She really looked beautiful; incredibly graceful in those fine clothes.

'I'm going to do the puja ceremony,' she said. 'Have you heard of it?'

I had. At least I had read about it in my *Lonely Planet*.

'Do you mind if I watch you?' I asked.

'OK.'

She led the way out of the front door and I saw the family shrine for the first time. It was set on a plinth in a shady corner, a sort of mini temple about the size of a doll's house.

Shreeya began by chanting a few mantras, inviting the gods to attend the ritual. While she sang I noticed that there were several photographs stuck inside the shrine, faded snapshots of old folk – presumably relatives.

But one of the photographs was different and Shreeya

paid it special attention as she performed the ritual, unpinning it to hold it tightly in her hand.

The picture was a colour print showing a handsome young Sherpa boy, perhaps fifteen or sixteen years old. He was pictured wearing mountain gear, standing in a place which looked snowy and wild.

He was a climber. No doubt about that. But what were the prayers Shreeya was offering for him?

Prayers for a soul already gone? Or prayers for his safety as he climbed?

When the chanting had ended Shreeya picked up a small brass hand bell with a carved wooden handle.

'The shrine bell,' she told me. 'The ceremony isn't over until the bell is rung.'

The bell rang clear as she shook it, the sound telling everyone that the puja had been successfully performed.

She pinned the photograph of the young climber back and I couldn't hold my curiosity any longer.

'Shreeya, can I ask you something?'

She nodded.

'Who is the boy in the picture? You seemed to be praying for him.'

Shreeya went silent for a while, then said, 'He is my friend. His name is Kami.'

'Ah. Well I hope I will meet him.'

Shreeya thought about this carefully, a strange fleeting confusion clouding her eyes.

'I don't know if that is possible. You see I do not know if any of us will see him again … nobody really knows if he is dead or alive.'

'Oh, I'm sorry.'

I didn't want to push it further; Shreeya was clearly reluctant to talk about her friend and I didn't want to upset her. But what had she meant? Had he left the village? Gone to study in India perhaps? Or had he been lost on a mountain trip?

It was a mysterious thing to say.

O

We spent the rest of the morning getting the medical gear down to the clinic. Dhorjee had dumped his rucksack there the previous evening so, miraculously, everything had arrived in one piece.

I was shocked by the state of the place. Paint was peeling from every wall, there was abundant mildew, and two of the windows were cracked.

We spent a couple of hours cleaning dead beetles out of the cupboards before a bunch of local dignitaries turned up to welcome me.

The speeches began.

The sun blazed harder.

It was during this ceremony that I began to feel rough. I shivered as my skin became chilled. The faint desire to vomit began to nag away but I knew I could not interrupt the ceremony and nor could I move out of the sun.

I kept smiling and gritted my teeth.

I was asked to say a few words but my tongue was swelling horribly, my spit thickening in that repulsive way it does just before you are sick.

I stopped the speech and sprinted for the nearest bushes where I retched long and hard.

'I think I might have picked up a bug in Kathmandu,' I told the villagers as I stumbled back out into the blazing sun.

It was a bit of a downer to say the least.

By nightfall I was back in my room at Shreeya's house, wrapped up in my sleeping bag and feeling pretty sorry for myself.

'You are shivering,' Shreeya said that night. Her aunt's watchful eyes stared at me without sympathy.

'Just some virus,' I told her. 'I'll be all right in the morning.'

I wasn't all right in the morning. In fact the fever had got worse and I now had deep muscle aches.

Shreeya watched over me as I lay there sweating in the sleeping bag. I treated myself with paracetamol and decided that it was probably a virulent case of flu. Or perhaps a gastric infection I had picked up during the week in Kathmandu.

Then, having been feverish for twenty-four hours, it suddenly got much worse and a stabbing pain started up in my chest.

'Maybe you need to go back to Kathmandu,' Shreeya suggested. 'Go to hospital.'

I knew she was right but there was no way I could trek back out along that path.

The high point that second day on my thermometer was 39.8 degrees, which felt pretty extreme. Shreeya was getting more and more concerned about the state of me and from that moment on she never left my side, holding cool damp cloths to my forehead in an attempt to break down the fever.

The pain in my chest was a give away and I now realised I had pneumonia, a lung infection almost certainly caused by the freezing rain and exhaustion of the trek. Every time I breathed I got this dagger stab of pain which felt like someone was twisting a Kitchen Devil into my ribs.

I was gobsmacked to be so sick. I was young. I was fit.

I had never had a serious illness in my life. But my travellers' medical handbook put me right; you can get pneumonia at any age, it said. Sometimes these things happen.

That night was the crisis. I was really in a state.

It got so bad that Shreeya actually put up a small shrine next to my bed. Incense was lit and she sat cross-legged in prayer as she watched over me.

Then, at the height of the fever, when I was almost delirious, Shreeya did the strangest thing.

She took the photograph of her friend Kami and put it to my chest. Like it was some sort of charm, or held some sort of spiritual power. She held it there tightly, still muttering a prayer as I struggled to breathe.

And the strangest thing of all was that it did have a result. At the very moment she was pressing the photograph to my body I sensed the pain in my chest beginning to ease off. For the first time in many hours I found myself able to breathe properly and the feeling of relief was almost overwhelming.

Shreeya took away the photograph and placed it on the makeshift shrine. Her eyes were glittering with an internal light. She rang the small shrine bell as a way of communicating thanks to the gods and she told me gently, 'I gave this shrine bell to my friend when he went to

Everest. It was returned to me after the expedition, with no explanation about what happened to him.'

Her words haunted me for hours. It seemed terrible not to know the fate of a loved one.

At long last I fell into a weird sleep, filled with bad dreams. In one nightmare I was engulfed by an avalanche on some huge mountain. Buried in the snow I heard scraping sounds. Then came a face, smiling at me. My saviour.

It was Kami – the boy from the picture.

I woke with a start, sitting up fast as my chest muscles tightened up.

I leaned over and picked up the photograph of Shreeya's friend. I felt an odd connection to him now, and was much more curious than before.

That morning the daily routines of the house went on around me. The buffalo were taken to the fields. The fire was lit in the room next door, the tinder crackling as it flared up. I heard the swish of Shreeya sweeping the floor with a hazel broom.

I thought about how generous Shreeya had been to me. I was a stranger to her really but she had shown me the most incredible hospitality and care, even if her aunt had shown little interest in my problems.

That night a nasty argument flared up between Shreeya

and her aunt. I had no idea what it was about but it ended with the sound of a slap or two and I heard Shreeya sobbing. Later, when things had calmed down a bit, I was strong enough to join them for supper.

Shreeya had a dark bruise on her cheek.

'You've been so kind,' I told her. 'What can I ever do to repay you?'

Shreeya looked at her aunt, a stare of pure defiance. The aunt just gave her a poisonous look by return and swept out of the kitchen.

'I want you to make a journey,' Shreeya told me earnestly. 'I need you to find out the truth about Kami.'

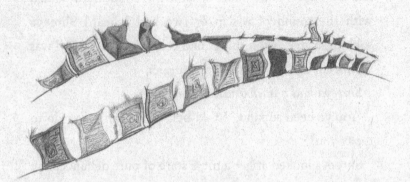

CHAPTER 2

It took me quite a few days to recover from my illness, but over the next four weeks the work at the village was done. We did a total refurb on the clinic, whitewashing the whole building and fixing the dodgy tiles on the roof.

From time to time I had been asking around amongst the elders of the village, checking whether they knew anything about the fate of Shreeya's friend Kami.

But all I got was rumours and half-baked theories. Some had heard whispers about a Sherpa boy that had been kidnapped by 'djinns' – the spirits of the mountains. Others repeated the rumour that he was 'neither dead or alive'.

It was strange how many people believed that.

I questioned Shreeya further about it but didn't get anything new. Her friend Kami had gone to Everest, something terrible had happened and she had been immediately spirited away to this remote corner of Nepal by her parents.

'I caused them shame,' she told me, 'and they have made me a prisoner here.'

I was pretty sure there was a side of the story that she was keeping from me. To be honest, I was beginning to give up on the idea of helping Shreeya find her friend. Of course that was the exact moment when Shreeya surprised me by producing a scrap of paper with the name 'Nima Gyaltsen' written on it.

A clue.

A lead.

'He lives in Aiselukharka village,' Shreeya told me. 'They say he was on the expedition with Kami.'

That was more like it. At least I had something to go on. That night I checked my map and found that the village mentioned in Shreeya's note was two hard days' trekking away.

I was planning to use my free days for a trek anyway, so I reckoned I might as well find a porter, head out to that village, and see if I could track down this Nima Gyaltsen character.

I packed up my rucksack and left the next morning, but only after Shreeya and some of the others blessed my journey with a long and touching puja ceremony. I had only been there for a short while but I was genuinely fond of her and the other villagers.

'I hope you will be back very soon,' Shreeya told me, 'with news of my friend.'

'I hope so too.'

O

As the friendly farewell calls of the watching villagers fell away, I soon found I had a real spring in my stride. Getting to the village where I would find the contact would involve a spectacular trek through amazing Himalayan scenery. Even better, I had a great porter with me this time. His name was Pasang and he seemed trustworthy and kind.

One of the main reasons I liked him was that he had a pair of red tartan socks that poked out of a gaping hole in the front of his boots.

At that point I was pretty sure of cracking the mission quickly. This guy Nima had actually been on the expedition with Kami. Surely he would be able to fill me in on what had happened and where he was? All I had to do was find Nima and the mystery would be solved.

At least that was what my brain was telling me.

On the first day we passed through quite a few small villages, almost all of them devoted to forestry and all of them poor. There were no rice mills here, no plump-looking water buffalo, just skinny chickens, fields of stunted beans and bad-tempered feral dogs.

We slept that night in a small tea house on mattresses that were infested with fleas. I itched my way through the night, regretting that I hadn't pitched my little one-man tent and slept outside. It would have been a better night.

Next day I really felt like we were walking off the edge of the map. The land became even more thickly forested, the valley sides steep and scarred with landslides.

The trek was long and it stretched me, just like the one to Shreeya's village, but not in such a brutal way. When we finally found the village where this man Nima lived, it was only the second place we had seen that day.

It was a bit of a dump really, an old army patrol post which had been abandoned by the military and squatted in ever since by hunters, berry pickers and brewers of chang – the local rice wine.

Pasang asked around for Nima and we quickly found someone who knew him. 'He'll be in the bar,' a friendly old woman told us, 'drinking, drinking.'

My heart sank as I heard this; I had already seen the damage that cheap alcohol could do in these small rural places and it seemed I was now in for another boozy encounter.

Pasang asked me to pay off his wages and let him return to his village. I did try to convince him to stick with me for another day but he had work waiting in his fields back home.

After he had gone I walked across to the bar, a rough and ready hovel which smelled to high heaven. There was no electric light, just a couple of candles, and it took a moment for my eyes to adjust as the five or six drinkers – all men – blinked at me in surprise.

I asked for Nima and was taken across to the darkest corner of the room where a figure was lying on a bench. He looked to be completely out of it, so I was surprised when he responded, more or less, to me calling his name.

'Whaaa? Who's that?' he cried in English. He lunged up from the shadows and crashed onto a nearby stool.

I could see that he was about eighteen years old, although his face was ravaged by cheap alcohol.

By the light of my torch I then saw something shocking; he had lost all the fingers on one hand and I guessed it was to frostbite. There was a rotten smell coming from him and I immediately suspected that his wounds had gone bad.

I said 'hi' in a friendly way but he just stared at me with a blank expression so I changed tack.

'Can I see your hand, please? I might be able to help you.'

He held out the damaged hand and I almost gasped out loud. The frostbitten fingers looked like they'd been inexpertly amputated, the wounds were weeping and urgently in need of attention.

I've seen some pretty gruesome medical emergencies with my dad's cattle over the years but this was something else.

'How long has it been like this?' I asked him.

Nima just shrugged but his friend replied:

'Since he come back from Everest.'

'Everest!' Nima suddenly yelled, ripping the hand away and tucking it beneath his arm.

'He's crazy,' his friend added apologetically.

'I want to clean up that hand,' I offered. 'I have bandages and everything I need. It will help you a lot.'

'No!' Nima spun around and lurched back towards the shadows in the corner of the bar. But his friend grabbed him by the shoulder and turned him.

'Let him help you,' he told Nima angrily. 'He can do you some good.'

Nima swayed a bit, stared at me hesitantly, then walked slowly over and let me examine the wounds.

'Will you let me do it?' I asked him. He nodded.

I worked by the tungsten light of my head torch for almost an hour, cleaning up the wounds and putting on a fresh dressing. It was the most complicated first aid I'd ever done, but I reckon it was an OK job.

'The expedition gave him money to have a proper operation,' Nima's friend explained at one point, 'but he spend the money on something else!'

Hmmm. At least that explained the amateur amputation job. He probably spent that money on booze.

I rummaged in my pack and found the little pot of antibiotics the charity had given me for the trip. I knew they were good for general infections.

Nima accepted the plastic pot with a grunt and I bought him a Coke so he could wash down the first tablet. He seemed to have sobered up quite a bit during the clean-up operation and I now raised the subject that had brought me here.

'I'm looking for a climbing Sherpa called Kami,' I told him. 'He was on an Everest expedition with you.'

'Kami?' Nima said softly, 'I don't want to talk about Kami.'

'But you know what happened to him?'

Nima's eyes clouded over.

'They took me off the mountain. Halfway through expedition, when my fingers got frozen. Took me to the hospital in Khumjung. I wasn't there at the end when everything went bad.'

'But you must know something.'

'I know the gods were angry. That much is sure.'

'Was Kami injured? Did he get frostbite like you?'

'You'll have to ask the bosses that. The Sirdar maybe, the Westerners, they knew. They didn't tell us Sherpas anything in the end.'

'But do you know where I can find him?'

'Yes. I have heard them say where he is. Kami. The one who did *this*.'

He suddenly became angry and irrational again, thrusting out his bandaged hand, displaying the sawn-off fingers angrily.

'His fault! Kami's fault.'

I flinched at this, wondering what he was really trying to tell me. I couldn't imagine for a second that Shreeya's friend might really be responsible for those awful wounds.

Or was he?

And if so, *how* was he responsible?

I brought out my large scale map of the region and folded it out across the pool table. The bar owner plonked a few candles on top of it, spilling molten wax onto the paper in his drunken haste.

Nima took a few moments to orientate himself to the map, tracing valley systems and finding villages with the shaking index finger of his good right hand.

'Here. That's where they said. This valley.'

He pointed at a remote spot, far from any habitation.

'But there's no village. You must be mistaken.'

'No,' Nima was insistent, 'he is here. Sure.'

I stared at the map, wondering whether Nima was taking the mickey. I was at a loss to think what anyone could be doing in such a place.

Then I got an idea.

'He lives alone? Has he become a monk?' I knew that there were many thousands of religious retreats dotted all about the mountains of Nepal.

Nima replied uncertainly, 'Maybe. Maybe.'

It seemed the most likely explanation.

'How many days' walk is that?' I asked the onlookers.

'Three days,' came the reply. 'Two nights sleeping if you are fast.'

I left the bar at about nine and pitched my tent. I was thinking about Nima and what a sad encounter it had been.

I suspected that he knew more about the reasons for

Kami's exile than he was letting on. So many hints and pointers but never that one clear piece of information which would explain the situation. But he *had* given me a further clue and for that I was grateful.

It *was* possible that Kami was holed up in some isolated little monastery. If something terrible had happened to him on the expedition then that might be a logical step for him to take. Retreat from the world. Give up his worldly life.

Now I had to make a fast decision. I had eight days of my holiday left.

The clock was ticking.

One thing was for sure: the only way I could really crack this mystery was to meet Kami face to face.

O

I was up at first light and I quickly decided to make the trek without a porter. The map was clear enough and I reckoned I could trust it.

Going solo was an exhilarating thought; so much so that I was really wired about it. I filled up my water bottles, packed my tent and hit the trail mid-morning.

The pack was a bit of a monster, thirty kilos at a guess – mostly thanks to the extra water – but by adjusting the chest and waist straps I could bear it all right.

The trail rose gently, dead centre on the valley floor, cutting through ancient forests of birch and juniper. For the first time since my illness I felt myself in good shape. My legs were strong and I was taking just five minutes rest for each hour of trekking.

Three hours of tramping brought me to a high bluff which formed the watershed with the next valley system. It almost looked like a scene from a Scottish glen, with fir trees scratching the skyline and ground cover of tough, wiry heathers.

I trekked on through the afternoon and as the sun started to set I began to look for a place to camp. There wasn't much flat ground, but I eventually found a little scoop of land which could just about take my tent.

Food was basic; just a few of the lentil and rice balls that Shreeya had given me for the journey and a cup of sweet tea. By the time I was done it was only half past six and the night was looking like it was going to be a long one.

Luckily I still had half a book to read, but it wasn't easy to concentrate.

The problem was this: with my head torch blazing inside, the tent shone like a lighthouse. For insects this strange glow was irresistible. They zoomed out of the darkness, beating themselves against the tent in a frenzy, humming and buzzing as they fought to get inside.

A few of them actually did get in through the tiny ventilation holes, looping the loop around my head like drunken aviators and crackling against my cheeks.

Squashing them was really nasty. It left a teaspoon of squidgy green gunk on the tent floor.

I didn't read for long.

O

Next day was drizzly and grey. The trees dripped with snotty dew and the moss was squelchy underfoot. I heated water and made myself a fast coffee, following it down with some crackers and dried apricots.

I met two people that morning: a hunter with the carcass of a young deer nestling on his shoulders and a woman with a woven basket filled with dark blue berries. She offered me a handful of the fruit, but it looked like deadly nightshade and I didn't have the nerve to try it. But we parted as friends after I gave her some sugar tied up in a wrap of paper.

There was less running water about so I began to take more care with my supplies. I rationed myself to a cupful every hour or so, and filled the canteens whenever I could.

Pretty soon things began to change. The track had a sinister vibe to it, narrowing and twisting in a most annoying way through swampy land, endless thorny brushwood and tangled knots of vines.

Next time I stopped I saw the leeches.

Leeches.

Vampire worms.

Five or six of them were fixed to my bare legs and I could feel one feeding behind my ear. Each was as long and thick as my index finger; their slick pulpy bodies pulsating as they sucked.

I felt a bit sick just looking at them.

I was desperate to rip the bloodsuckers off by sheer force but I knew it would only make matters worse. The mouth parts would be left to fester in the wound, risking infection.

Finally, I cracked open my little medical kit and found a bottle of medical iodine. I squirted a few drops onto the business end of one of the bigger leeches and after a few seconds I was able to pull it off. In this way I removed more than eight of the creatures. The bite wounds bled like mad, but I cleaned them and stuck a waterproof plaster on each. That was the best I could do.

The march continued with me taking much more care now not to brush my body against the overhanging branches. I was pretty knackered that afternoon, so I pitched camp early, falling asleep at about 7 p.m. and sleeping like a log right through the dark hours.

Next morning I hit the trail early. It had been a thirsty night and I really needed to find fresh water. I trekked for a few hours before finally finding a small spring where I could fill up. The wait for the chlorine tablets to kick in seemed endless.

Fifteen minutes is a long time when your mouth is dry as dust.

As I drank my fill I noticed a huge collection of boulders lying at the valley side. I scrambled up onto the rocks. It was a rare opportunity to see across the landscape. I rubbed sweat out of my eyes and realised with a sense of weary satisfaction that my search was almost over.

Across the valley I could see the outline of a building, set tight against the cliffs on the far side.

That had to be the place that Nima had mentioned. A number of trees were planted about it but I could still see enough to pick out the outline of a small bungalow with a corrugated tin roof.

I followed the trail down to the valley floor and plodded for an hour or more through thickets of wild bamboo. The track began to rise again. I was getting really close to the building now and I began to notice a faint mechanical hum.

I gradually realised that there was a generator up there,

buzzing away. When I thought about it, it seemed a bit odd; where would they get the fuel from in a place like this? And who would pay for such a high cost item here in one of the poorest countries in the world?

Another little mystery to add to the list.

Twenty minutes later I hauled myself round a final switch-back and arrived at a wall which marked the boundary of the compound.

I followed the wall around and reached a rough tin door. Then – with a warning call of 'Hello!' – I pushed it open and entered, hoping there would be no guard dog to welcome me.

The compound was neat and tidy, the bungalow showing signs of a recent paint job. The windows facing me were partly open, their dark green shutters swung wide to profit from the late afternoon sun.

I repeated my call, adding 'anybody around?'

Still no reply.

Suddenly, out of the corner of my eye, I caught movement to the side of the bungalow, fifty metres away at the foot of the cliff.

It seemed that someone was there, deep in the forest canopy, but that they had ducked out of sight upon seeing me. I stared long into the dark shadows but nothing further moved.

Maybe I had been mistaken.

I was about to walk right up to the front door when I heard noise coming from the far end of the building.

I walked around and found an old man working in the garden. He was a fit-looking character with a full head of silver hair, a neatly trimmed silver beard and a stained pair of gardening dungarees.

'Hi! Erm, Namaste.'

My greeting caught the man by surprise. He stopped his weeding, jerked his head up and stared at me with his mouth open.

'Oh!' He looked me up and down with astonishment.

'I'm sorry to disturb you,' I told him, feeling guilty to have given him such a shock.

He continued to stand there, clutching the hoe, frozen to the spot, struck dumb by this unexpected arrival.

'I'm looking for someone called Kami,' I said.

'Are you a journalist?' he asked me suspiciously. 'I have been warned that journalists may one day come.'

'Actually I'm working with a charity,' I told him. 'I've been helping out at the clinic at Tanche village.'

At the mention of the village name his eyes narrowed a bit. I decided I had to establish some basics.

'He was a climbing Sherpa,' I explained. 'Have I come to the right place?'

The man didn't try to answer this and his stern gaze was starting to get to me. Old doubts about the nature of this mad trip flooded back and I felt foolish and a bit lost.

Then he smiled. It was as if he had, in that moment, decided that I was OK.

'Would you like some tea?' he asked.

Breakthrough.

I nodded and thanked him.

'This way.'

The old man led me towards a bamboo hut which had been built as a lean-to at the back of the building. A little fire was smouldering in the middle of the dirt floor and he snapped some twigs to feed it.

I introduced myself.

'Dawa,' he told me by return.

He stoked up some coals and prepared the tea with calm movements, selecting the tea leaves and sugar from ancient tins which had long ago lost their labels.

'Is that a generator I can hear?' I asked him. Dawa nodded. 'How do you keep it going?'

'There are porters,' the old man said. 'They come at the beginning of each month, bringing food and fuel for myself, for Kami and for the … carer … '

'Carer?' I asked him. Dawa did not reply to that question. Instead, after a long pause he fired back with: 'Who told you about this place?'

'A climbing Sherpa called Nima. He was once on an expedition with Kami.'

Dawa poured the amber-coloured liquid from on high. It splashed into the tiny glasses and the pleasing smell of the tea filled the little hut.

'What did they tell you about him?'

'Not much. But there seems to be this legend that he is neither dead nor alive.'

'Ha!' Dawa laughed, 'There are many superstitious people out there. He is most certainly alive but I can tell you nothing else. I have been sworn to say no more.'

We sipped the tea, my body craving the sugars after the long trek. I decided to go for the jugular.

'Can I see him?'

Dawa thought for a while.

'That will depend,' he replied cryptically. 'If you are prepared to *wait*, then maybe.'

These words plunged me into an instant depression. I would have to wait? For how *long* would I have to wait? *And why?*

In any case I would have to be back in Kathmandu sometime before the week was out, so it wasn't as if I had a load of slack in my diary.

'Can you give me an idea of how long?' I pleaded.

'I cannot say,' he told me, finally. 'It is not for me to decide.'

I was confused about this iffy welcome and more than a little bit fed up by it. This guy Dawa seemed to be hinting that it might be days before I was allowed to see Kami, or that I might not be able to see him at all.

But what would it depend on? My behaviour? On the word of the gods? On Kami himself? Or on the carer that Dawa had mentioned?

Come to that, where was the carer? Perhaps that fleeting figure I had seen near the foot of the cliff had been him? Or her?

The whole thing was unsettling, in fact, downright weird.

I put up my tent on the only flat ground available, a mean scrap of swampy grass next to the spring.

Out in the musty forest a nightjar was celebrating all through the dark hours, liquid notes mingling with dreams which were surprisingly pleasant.

O

The next morning passed quickly enough. I hung the sleeping

bag up to air and borrowed a plastic tub and some soap from Dawa. A clean-up session was overdue. It was time to wash my sweat-encrusted clothes – and my body too.

As I began to wash, everything seemed to go quiet.

Once again, I got the strangest feeling.

The sensation of being watched.

I spun around quickly, fixing my gaze on the nearest patch of dense forest, feeling sure I would see someone, eyes staring out at me from that green refuge. But there was no one.

At least no one I could see.

'Who's there?' I called softly, getting no reply apart from the drone of the cicadas.

I walked slowly in amongst the trees, the birds trilling alarm calls at the invasion. I went on, deeper, pushing through clinging vegetation. The birds fell suddenly silent, all I could hear was the drip, drip of soapy water falling from the T-shirt I was carrying.

Still I felt it.

Someone is here.

I stared into the forest depth where every shadow seemed to have human form.

'Hello?'

Nothing. Now I felt foolish and I went back to the glade and finished the washing.

Focus on practical stuff. You're just tired and a bit messed up from the trek.

Dawa called me in for lunch, a tasty curry of chickpeas and spinach served with gritty brown rice. We ate it from aluminium dishes, cross-legged on the dirt floor of his shack while he told me about the time he served with the Ghurka regiment.

'Twenty-five years serving Her Majesty the Queen,' he said with pride. 'Oman, Belize, Borneo. All over the world.'

I worked in the garden all through the afternoon, partly to repay Dawa for the lunch but also because there was little else to do. I pulled and washed two baskets of plump carrots and cleaned a sackful of weeds from a derelict patch at the side of the house.

The shutters were closed and I could see nothing of the interior. I placed my ear to one of them, but all I could hear was the whirr of machines from inside.

The second day passed in much the same way: two back-breaking sessions in the garden followed by an evening spent in Dawa's shack, listening to the BBC World Service on his vintage transistor radio.

'Wars everywhere!' Dawa exclaimed in disgust. 'One war stops. Another one starts.'

On the morning of the third day I could sense that something was different. Dawa disappeared into the bungalow and left me to my own devices. I wrote up my diary and sunbathed for a bit, then scraped the stubble off my chin with a blunt disposable razor I found in the bottom of my washbag.

I was just thinking of going for a walk in the forest when Dawa came back looking pleased with himself.

'Follow me,' he said with a smile. 'You do not have to wait any more.'

We walked together to the front door of the bungalow. From there we passed down a short corridor, then entered a room which was part bedroom, part hospital ward. I was in a bit of a daze at this point, and I blinked in amazement at the white-painted room which was stuffed with gently humming medical machines.

In the corner of the room, lit by soft sunlight filtering through wooden shutters, I saw Kami for the first time. He was dressed in a striking pair of red and white striped pyjamas and lying in a high-tech bed which seemed to be rocking in gentle waves. A second or two later – with a disturbing shock – I recognised it as the type of device used to stop paralysed patients from getting bed sores. I'd seen similar beds when I'd done my work experience at the local hospital back home.

'Welcome!' Kami's voice was eager and strong. He was obviously very excited to have a visitor.

I approached the bed and we stared at each other for a while, both grinning like idiots at the pleasure of the encounter. For me it was the sense of accomplishing a task; I had taken on this quest for Shreeya and had not failed her. For him, I guessed, it was the opportunity to talk to someone new. I reached out to clutch his hand, holding it tight for a few seconds in the universal way of greeting.

He did not grip my hand back. In fact, his entire body seemed strangely motionless from the neck down, his muscles evidently atrophied.

That's when I got it.

Kami was paralysed from the neck down.

A boy who is neither dead nor alive.

Suddenly those rumours were making a terrible sort of sense.

Probably, I reckoned, he had broken his spine: an injury that would leave him paralysed for life even though he could obviously move his head a bit and breathe without a machine.

I was gutted to see the situation he was in and I immediately wondered how on earth Shreeya would react to the news.

A whole load of questions zapped through my mind.

What accident had he had? Who had paid for this place to be built? Where was the mystery carer that Dawa had mentioned?

But I didn't have a chance to dwell on any of these things because Kami's face broke out into the most brilliant smile as I sat in the chair next to him. He was every bit as handsome as the photograph that Shreeya still cherished – and definitely still filled with a zest for life. He turned his head a little and regarded me as if I was a visiting angel.

We really did have an amazing and instant connection between us. I have never liked someone so fast in my life. I was intensely curious to find out more about him.

'You cut yourself,' Kami told me with a smile. His eyes were locked on my chin.

'Oh … I just shaved.' I took out a tissue and dabbed at the bloodspot.

'Have you got news from Shreeya?'

'Yes. It was Shreeya that sent me to try and find you.'

This provoked a sort of gasp from Kami and he turned his face away. A single tear ran down his cheek and he breathed deeply for a minute or two as he recovered his composure.

'I will leave you both,' Dawa said tactfully.

He softly closed the door.

And that was when Kami began to talk.

CHAPTER 3

Kami's Story

It was a crisp November morning, a rare day of calm punctuating the turbulence of the Himalayan winter. Kami and his father were high above the snowline, cutting trees by hand. A small billycan of tea was boiling up on an open fire nearby. A handful of potatoes were baking in the ashes, their deliciously earthy scent mingling with the wounded, resiny smell of freshly cut wood.

Back and forth swung the two-man saw, the sixteen-year-old Sherpa lad hardened to the labour by years of practice. There was a hypnotic quality to the work, he had come to realise, and he found he could lose himself in elaborate daydreams to dull the pain.

Most of his fantasies were about the big mountains.

Everest above all.

Then a voice called out nearby; a young boy from the village had run up with a message for Kami;

'There's a man come to see you from Namche Bazaar,' he said breathlessly. 'Says his name is Jamling.'

The tree gave up its fight with a rendering crack of splintering wood. Kami and his father had to jump for their lives as it fell.

The work was over for the day; the two of them washed in a nearby stream and followed the young boy down to the village where they found the smiling figure of Jamling waiting for them by the village shrine.

'Namaste,' he greeted them warmly.

'Namaste.'

Kami bowed deeply as a mark of respect.

The elderly Sherpa was well known in the village, his ever smiling face always a welcome presence in Kami's home. Kami and his father had met him some years before, on one of their trading trips to sell timber in Namche Bazaar and since that time he had become a firm family friend.

Jamling had been to the summit of Everest on five occasions and his scrapbook of photographs was an endless source of fascination to Kami. He had become something of a mentor to the young Sherpa boy, and had employed him the previous year as a trainee porter on a few short expeditions to local trekking peaks.

Kami had proved himself to be strong and reliable out on the trail and Jamling had given him some climbing training. He even paid for Kami to continue his English studies and bought him the textbooks his family could not otherwise afford.

'Come and share rice with us,' Kami's father insisted.

Jamling accepted the invitation and followed the two to the house where Kami's mother and sister had already prepared lentils and curried potatoes in his honour.

Being the most senior person present, the visitor performed a small ritual of thanks before they ate, sprinkling a few grains of rice and water on the mud floor of the kitchen and thanking the gods for their generosity.

As he performed this task Kami noticed that three of Jamling's fingers on his right hand were now little more than stumps. He wasn't surprised at this new injury; frostbite was quite common amongst the men of Namche Bazaar, especially those who went high with the climbing expeditions.

The men ate in silence, Kami wondering with barely suppressed excitement what the purpose of the visit could be.

For some years he had dreamed of working with one of the big expeditions. Jamling had often dropped hints that he would consider Kami for his high altitude climbs, but until now he had evidently considered the boy too young.

But now? Maybe the time had come.

When the rice was finished, tea was brought in. The men sipped it appreciatively and finally Jamling judged it a decent moment to speak his business.

'I'm looking for an assistant,' he said at last, 'an expedition to Everest next spring. We'll be helping an American politician to get to the summit. Three months.'

Everest!

The very word seemed to be loaded with a spectacular type of magic. Kami had to bite his tongue to stop himself crying out with joy. An invitation to work on an expedition was one thing but this was the ultimate!

'Ah,' Kami's father nodded calmly but his mother looked away and Kami could see the shadow across her face. She was alert to the dangers inherent in such a proposal; everyone in the Khumbu knew a family who had lost a loved one to the big mountains.

'What would the duties be?' his father asked.

'General stuff,' Jamling replied, 'looking after the yaks, helping to set up Base Camp and so on.'

'Will I be part of the climbing team?' Kami asked, his heart pounding away crazily at the very thought of such an honour.

'That depends on a great many things,' Jamling replied thoughtfully, 'and the final decision will be with the Sirdar ...'

The room went quiet as the family digested this.

'But I think you would be strong enough to carry loads on the mountain,' Jamling continued, more encouragingly. 'And you already know most of the climbing techniques.'

'What would the pay be?' his father asked.

'Twelve dollars a day.'

Kami did a quick calculation in his head. Twelve dollars a day for ninety days ... came to more than a thousand dollars. If he was careful not to spend it, he would come out of the expedition with a small fortune by local standards.

He would be earning more cash in three months than his father could make in the same period through cutting and selling timber. It was a peculiar thought and in a way it made Kami sad. A lifetime of backbreaking labour had given his father no financial security at all; the family had always lived hand-to-mouth.

'What about clothing?' his father asked. 'The special gear he will need?'

'Everything will be provided,' Jamling said. 'Down jacket, proper boots, glacier goggles, the works. If the Sirdar likes you he'll let you keep it all at the end as a bonus.'

Kami was thrilled to hear this.

'You will have to train,' Jamling warned, 'all through the winter. There's no room for slackers on these expeditions.'

'I won't let you down,' Kami told him earnestly.

Jamling nodded at this and then showed Kami a magazine article about the 'boss' of the forthcoming expedition, an American senator by the name of Alex Brennan. The pictures showed a handsome middle-aged man with a flowing mane of blonde hair. Kami thought he looked more like a surfer or rock star than a politician.

Kami quickly scanned the article, learning that Brennan had big ideas for America; he had written passionate articles against war and won the hearts of millions of ordinary people with his proposals for a fairer government.

'He's an amazing man,' Jamling told them. 'He rowed for the USA Olympic team when he was at college, loves to climb, loves to explore his own limits. They say he may one day be the President of the United States so we have to make sure he gets back from Everest in one piece!'

And with that the venerable Sherpa was done. He finished his tea and respectfully bade the family farewell.

Kami could barely sleep that night. He was wound up with excitement at the events of the day.

The invitation from Jamling was thrilling enough but that wasn't the only reason that Kami saw this as a priceless opportunity.

This wasn't just about the mountain. There was a problem in Kami's life that he really needed to solve.

And Everest might give him a way to do it.

O

When he was eight years old, Kami had been put through a ceremony in which he was 'married' to a girl from a neighbouring village.

Her name was Laxmi. She was six, and he had never seen her in his life before.

Child marriages like this were quite rare amongst the Sherpa people, but Kami's mother was from the south-west of Nepal where the custom was still fairly common. She had persuaded Kami's father that the 'marriage' should go ahead.

Kami still had some faint memories of the ceremony: his mother bathing him in a perfumed tub of warm water, the suit of finest cloth that he was forced to wear, the rich red dress and glinting of gold coins worn by his nervous 'bride'.

Incense was burned, musicians played Dhimay drums late into the night and a great deal of Rakshi was drunk by the men.

The family of the bride paid a dowry to Kami's father, a sum measured in many thousands of rupees. The deal was done. The pact solemnised by a holy man. Kami and Laxmi would one day live together as man and wife, raise a family together and live happily ever after.

At the time Kami was barely aware of the significance of the ceremony. Such a 'marriage' was seen more as a social pact between two families, a way of strengthening ties between villages.

The fact that it was technically illegal under Nepali law was of no concern at all.

The ceremony was nothing but a faded memory to Kami, but now the clock was ticking. He had recently turned sixteen, his 'bride' was fourteen, and pressure was already beginning to kick in. Word had reached him that Laxmi had gone through her coming of age ritual to mark her first menstruation.

In the eyes of her family she was ready to become Kami's wife for real. And they had the right to insist on it.

'When is your son coming for Laxmi?' her father enquired sharply of Kami's father when they met at the local market. 'People are beginning to talk. I do not want my daughter to suffer any shame.'

Kami's father had long dreaded this encounter. He knew full well that the time had come for Kami to bring Laxmi back to his family home.

'I will talk to the boy,' he assured Laxmi's father. 'Things will happen soon.'

Laxmi's father nodded gracefully but there was an unmistakeable gleam of doubt in his eyes.

And Kami's father knew why.

The reason for that gleam of doubt was Kami's relationship with a girl from his own village. Her name was Shreeya and she had been a friend and companion to Kami since he was old enough to roam around the village on his own.

Shreeya was a little younger than Kami. She had a quicksilver laugh and a secret desire to be an actress. Although she seemed shy and timid in public, in private she could be a wicked mimic, able to imitate the tremulous, quavering tones of the village elders in a way that could have other kids in stitches.

She had curiosity for everything, excelling at school where she was effortlessly the most talented pupil in her class. Like Kami she was a good linguist, and had mastered English easily.

Shreeya and Kami had shared some extraordinary adventures, mainly thanks to the honey hunting expeditions of her father. Shreeya had always been enthralled by his tales of river crossings on rickety old rope bridges and of freezing cold nights camped in the shadow of mighty glaciers.

'Take me with you,' she begged. But her father merely laughed and told her it was man's work.

Finally, when she had turned fourteen, Shreeya's father told her she could accompany him on one of the journeys. She immediately asked if her friend Kami could come along too.

'He can come if he's prepared to help me carry the honey,' her father said with a smile. 'That's a twenty-kilo jerrycan in each hand.'

Kami was thrilled to get the invitation. He wasn't afraid of hard work and he was already strong as an ox from the forestry work with his father.

They left at dawn one fine August day, trekking towards the Langtang district where the wild bees could be found. As the sun went down, Shreeya's father would light a small fire and put water to boil. Rice was cooked with spicy sauce. For dessert they would eat handfuls of wild strawberries or blackberries they found along the trail.

After two days on the trek they reached wild valleys

which were packed with alpine flowers.

'You see that?' Shreeya's father pointed to a fawn-coloured object high on a cliff. 'That's one of the nests. The bees are smart. They build them out of reach of the bears.'

Then the harvesting began and for the first time Shreeya and Kami understood the incredible risks involved. In some places, ancient bamboo ladders were already in place. In new locations her father cut fresh bamboo in the forest and built ladders of his own. He would light a fire, create a core of glowing coals, and then clamber up those precipitous cliffs with a metal can of the smouldering embers.

'The smoke calms them down,' he told them, but it hardly seemed to be true.

Once he was up there, he would attack the nest with a special tool – a long pole with a curved blade set into the end. As soon as the knife began to cut into the honeycomb, the furious insects would go into a frenzy, flying into the air and attacking en masse.

'Here comes a big bit!' he would scream down.

Kami and Shreeya would run to catch the honeycomb before it hit the ground. Seeing her father disappear beneath a swirling swarm of bees was a heart-stopping sight for Shreeya; on occasions she could hardly see him for the black cloud of insects. Time and again he would hack at the hive, cleaving dripping chunks of honeycomb off as fast as he could.

'Let me see your arms,' Shreeya said after one honey raid.

Her father reluctantly pulled up his shirt sleeves to reveal a mass of livid red bumps. Sometimes the accumulation of bee venom would send him into a sort of shivering trance which could last an hour or more.

'You get half a kilo each a day!' he told them. The fresh honeycomb was the most delicious thing the children had ever tasted; an explosion of lavender and jasmine on the tongue.

By the third day of the trip they had harvested more than fifty kilos of honey and there was still space in the plastic jerrycans for another ten.

They passed a high mountain col and came to a wind-swept plateau, an outstandingly beautiful wilderness of meadows and glaciated peaks.

'We can camp here tonight,' he told the children. They put down their packs with relief, running to fill the water bottles at one of the natural springs that seeped from the valley wall.

High above the sacred lakes, in a separate, hidden-away valley, a series of limestone cliffs formed a scar in the mountainside. The location looked a good hunting ground for wild bees, Shreeya's father had decided, and the next day he led the children across another high pass to take a look.

As they approached the valley wall Shreeya suddenly froze. 'There's something moving' she said, pointing to the base of the cliffs, 'over there by the cave.'

The place she was pointing towards was many hundreds of metres away. Kami couldn't see anything there at all and nor could her father despite his sharp eyesight.

'What is it?' Kami asked.

'I don't know. Some sort of creature. Let's wait a while, see if it comes out of the rocks.'

The three of them ducked behind a bush and waited for a while.

'The wind is in our favour,' her father whispered. 'If there's something there it won't pick up our scent.'

'There it is again,' Shreeya whispered.

'I can see it!' Kami hissed excitedly.

'A snow leopard!' Shreeya's father whispered in awe. 'The first time I've seen one.'

The cat strutted out of the rocks with regal grace, the distinctive dark rosettes of its markings clearly visible against a fur that was somewhere between ivory and honey. The thick tail was raised high, moving sensually back and forth in a way that reminded Shreeya of a snake being charmed.

'Don't make a sound,' her father whispered. Shreeya hardly dared to breathe, so desperately did she want this moment to continue.

The cat prowled about the meadow, seeming to check the terrain. Even at that distance, Kami could see the latent power of this rare cat. Every movement it made was filled with a glorious grace and strength.

Having made a tour of inspection, the leopard began to call, a curiously high pitched 'chuffing' sound which was somewhere between a cry and a sneeze. An answering bleat came from the rocks and the children held their breath as a young cub moved cautiously out of cover to join its mother. It mewled a greeting and nuzzled against her cheek as she licked at its fur.

'There's a second!' Shreeya whispered. Her sharp eyes once again the first to spot the movement.

A few moments later the second snow leopard cub crept with elaborate care out of the rocks.

'Keep totally still,' Shreeya's father whispered.

The three of them held their breaths as the leopard scanned the scree slopes, ever vigilant, ever wary of any threat to her cubs. At one point she seemed to look directly at them, but they were well-hidden behind the bush and the creature began to relax as she suckled her cubs.

They fed for several minutes before becoming restless. The two cubs struck off on their own. Mewing and calling, they started to explore the meadow, sniffing at flowers and leaping up at butterflies.

The spectacle could have continued but a shrill cry in the sky above the meadow caused the mother leopard to take fright. A huge eagle had soared up the ridge, playing on the late afternoon thermals. The mother cat uttered an alarm cry as she saw this dangerous predator, an urgent barking noise which immediately caused her babies to rush to her side.

The three creatures leapt with liquid bounds across the meadow and disappeared amidst the boulders that littered the foot of the cliff.

The show was over and Shreeya's father decided it would be prudent to quit the area as quickly as they could.

'Better to leave the leopards in peace,' he said. 'If they see us they'll be forced to leave the den.'

They crossed another watershed and found a different area of cliffs in an adjoining valley, which provided the final ten kilos of honey they needed to make the trip a success.

During the trek home Shreeya talked incessantly about

the leopard encounter, re-living every moment and pestering her father to tell her everything he could about the cats.

'I'm going to be a warden when I grow up,' Shreeya announced proudly, 'and work for the national parks so I can see them whenever I like.'

Kami and her father laughed at this precocious proposition. But neither of them doubted her determination.

Back at the village Shreeya's father gave them five hundred rupees each out of the profit he made on the honey. Kami gave his to his father; Shreeya ordered a book from a shop in Kathmandu. It was a picture book about snow leopards, describing everything then known about the behaviour of that most elusive of Himalayan creatures.

She read it cover to cover, again and again, and it became her most treasured possession.

There were other memorable moments on that journey but Shreeya and Kami knew that the vision of those snow leopards playing on the meadow would stay with them for the rest of their lives.

O

Not long after the honey-collecting trip, in the dying days of that summer, a stranger arrived in the village. A furtive-looking character with sharp features and a mouth full of rotting teeth, he walked with a pronounced limp and his thigh was bandaged with a dirty strip of cotton.

Nobody knew where he had come from and he did not volunteer his name.

He just limped out of the forest carrying nothing but an ancient Remington rifle and a greasy hessian sack.

'He smells strange,' Kami told his father that night as they shared rice, 'like blood.'

'No good will come of him,' Kami's father said, and Kami experienced, for the first time in his life, the unsettling feeling that his father was afraid.

'Is he a bandit?' Kami asked. He had heard stories of the brigands who lived wild in some of the more remote valleys.

His father just shrugged. But he couldn't hide the disquiet in his face.

In fact the newcomer was a hunter, as became clear over the following days.

The man put the word out; he was on the lookout for many types of wild creatures, he told the villagers, particularly monkeys, deer and bears. He could sell the pelts for large sums in the markets of Kathmandu and certain glands and organs would be sold to a Chinese trader who specialised in traditional medicine.

He would pay good money for information which would

lead him to a kill, he promised them, and the biggest money of all would be for information which would put him on the trail of a snow leopard.

Snow leopard skins could fetch thousands of dollars on the black market, he told them. Collectors in Hong Kong and Beijing would fight to obtain them. Such a prize would have to be handled with great care, he warned, as government wardens were authorised to shoot poachers on sight.

He pulled down the bandage on his thigh and showed them an ugly scar. A bullet was still in there, he boasted, and he didn't want another to add to the collection.

Total secrecy was necessary.

Kami had listened in on one of these conversations and at the mention of killing snow leopards he felt a flush of anger overwhelm him. He ran to Shreeya and told her what the hunter was planning.

Shreeya was shocked to the core. The very thought that someone could want to kill such a beautiful creature was so alien to her that she struggled to believe it was true.

'Do you think he'll find out about the family we saw?'

'If he does it'll be a disaster,' Kami replied. 'Who else knows about them apart from your father and us?'

Shreeya shook her head. 'I don't know, but I can ask my

father who he has told.'

When they met next day Shreeya was looking gloomy.

'My father can't remember how many people he told,' she said. 'But he thinks maybe four or five.'

'Four or five?' Kami's heart sank at this news.

'But he says he won't give that man any information and neither will the others,' she told Kami. 'He says the man looks like a crook and nobody's going to trust him.'

'But maybe some others will want the money,' Kami suggested.

For the first few days Shreeya's father's theory was proved correct. The villagers were indeed initially reluctant to co-operate. But the hunter was persistent and cunning; he paid for millet wine to be brewed and invited some of the elders to join him for a drink.

'This village has been poor for too long,' he told them as the alcohol began to flow. 'It is time for you to make some money.'

The millet wine was potent enough to loosen a few tongues and after four or five glasses, inspired by the thought of the money they could make, the men began to talk. Many of them knew where rhesus monkeys could be found, others knew the glades where deer grazed in the early mornings.

Some had seen evidence of a bear in a region of forest less than one hour from the village.

And one knew of a family of snow leopards which lived in the cliffs above one of Langtang's sacred lakes.

At the mention of this last lead, the hunter smiled his rotten smile and became more generous than ever. Where was this lake, he asked. Which trail should he take to get there? Was it a solitary animal or a family?

The party went on until the early hours, laughter ringing out as those present celebrated the riches they would surely soon possess.

When the village woke up the next morning the hunter was gone.

○

News that the hunter had vanished spread rapidly around the village, and Kami and Shreeya soon found out that he had been told about the whereabouts of the snow leopard family.

The two children ran to Shreeya's father and delivered the bad news.

'We have to chase after him,' Shreeya begged. 'Can't you persuade some men to go with you?'

'It's not so easy as that,' her father protested. 'People

have to work. They haven't got time to rush around the forest for days on end.'

'Won't they want to save the leopards?' Shreeya found it hard to believe that anyone could sleep at night when such noble creatures were in danger.

'Think about it,' her father continued. 'That man is obviously a bad piece of work and he's armed with a gun. If he discovers he's being tracked then who knows what could happen ...'

The children shivered at these words. The idea of that feral man of the forest hiding in the shadows with a gun was indeed a terrifying one.

'What about the wildlife rangers?' Kami suggested. 'Can't we tell them what's happening?'

Shreeya's father considered this but then shook his head. 'The nearest ranger post is four days' walk away, and in the opposite direction. By the time we got there it would already be too late.'

'I wish we'd never seen them!' Shreeya cried. 'Then they'd be safe!'

Shreeya hated to cry, but on this occasion she couldn't hold back the tears. Her father held her tight, patting her head gently as she sobbed.

'How long will it take him to get there?' asked Kami.

Shreeya's father thought a few moments. 'With that leg it will probably take him three days and nights. And he'll have to stake out the cliffs when he arrives. He might have to wait a day or two to even see the leopards.'

'Then there *is* time to stop him, if we trek as fast as we can. Please father. I beg you.'

'I'm sorry,' he said. 'We're not going to do it and that's the end of the conversation. You'll just have to hope those leopards have moved somewhere else.'

'They won't have,' Shreeya said miserably, 'I read it in the book. The mother will keep the cubs in the same den all summer unless something disturbs them.'

At that point, a couple of visitors arrived, and Shreeya's father instructed Kami and Shreeya to fetch two jerrycans of water. They ran through the rice fields to the well and sat side by side on a stone wall as the containers slowly filled.

'I'll never forgive myself if those leopards get shot,' Shreeya said. 'It's really our fault.'

Then a light of hope entered her eyes as a daring new thought ran through her mind.

'What if we leave tonight? Just the two of us, trekking as fast as we can?'

Kami wondered if he had heard right.

'*What!?* Just the two of us? What are you talking about?

They'll never let us.'

'Who said we're going to ask them?'

'You're crazy!'

Kami knew that Shreeya was capable of being headstrong, impetuous sometimes, but on this occasion what she was proposing was little short of outrageous.

'Run away to Langtang without telling anyone? They'll catch us and we'll be beaten black and blue.'

'And if we don't the leopards will be shot.'

Kami looked at Shreeya. Her face was set and utterly determined; her eyes bright and filled with confidence. He had seen that look before, but never quite like this. He felt a thrilling shiver of excitement run through his body; the very air around Shreeya seemed to crackle with dangerous potential.

And most thrilling of all was the feeling that she really needed him at her side. This was something that she couldn't do alone.

'OK,' he said. 'Let's say we do it. Let's say we manage to get away and we make it to Langtang. What if he's already there? You want to get into a fight with a man with a gun?'

'We try and get there before him. Find a way to scare the leopards away.'

'But he's a day ahead already.'

'OK. So we'll trek day and night. We could probably do it in two days if we don't stop.'

Kami laughed out loud. This escapade was getting more radical by the minute. Getting to the Langtang cliffs in two days would make it a phenomenally hard trek and there were many hazards they would face on the way.

'You really think we can do that?' he asked.

'We have to do it. There's no choice,' she replied earnestly. And he knew she absolutely meant it.

Kami thought about it as they carried the water containers back up to the village. His mind was fogged up with adrenaline but he knew there was no time for weighing up the pros and cons; it was something they had to act on immediately or not at all.

Above all he couldn't let Shreeya down. By the time they had reached the village shrine he had made the decision.

'All right,' he told her, 'let's do it.'

The smile she gave him at that moment was enough to take Kami's breath away. At that same moment he noticed for the first time how her face had changed that summer. The soft lines of childhood were magically gone and the elegant shape of Shreeya's face was now that of a young woman ... and a beautiful one at that.

'We'll need food,' Shreeya said, ever practical. 'Get what

you can. I'll meet you at the shrine at midnight.'

And with that she took the heavy jerrycans and slipped away through the village streets.

Shreeya wrote a note in her school book that night and left it open where her father would find it.

We have gone to save the leopards. It said simply. *Please don't worry.*

Kami got busy as soon as his family were asleep, creeping from his bed and entering the kitchen. He found some boiled eggs, half a kilo of raisins and a few packets of biscuits. He opened up the front door with infinite care, cursing the huge wooden catch as it creaked and groaned.

Shreeya was already tucked into the shadows, waiting for him by the village shrine.

'Let's go.' Kami was itching to get away.

They slipped away from the village on a little-used track, dodging into the star-cast shadows of the night and grateful for a half moon of guiding light. Kami felt tenser than he had ever been in his life, his guts churning ceaselessly as he wondered if they would yet be caught.

With every step they feared a shout would ring out behind them, but all was quiet. Only the electric buzz of nocturnal insects and the liquid song of nightjars punctuated the silence.

After an hour of fast walking they reached the critical point on the trail; the place where they would have to turn off the main path and commit to the long climb up the valley wall.

'Last chance. You can go back if you want,' Shreeya told him earnestly. He could see her eyes glinting in the moonlight. 'You won't be missed if you go back now.'

Kami thought about it for a few moments. He knew full well that this escapade was going to put him in big trouble. It would earn him a beating at least, and possibly a long 'grounding' when he would be forbidden to leave the village.

But his loyalty to Shreeya was absolute, and he could not imagine letting her go on this perilous journey alone.

'I'm coming with you,' he said firmly, and the two of them stepped onto the trail that led upwards into the dark forest.

○

The further they got from the village the wilder the night became. Occasionally they disturbed foraging animals, jumping out of their skins as a wild pig or deer crashed away in a panic through the undergrowth.

At dawn the trail came to a river crossing that Shreeya

remembered badly from their previous journey. It was a rope bridge across a deep canyon and it swayed alarmingly; Shreeya was nervous of heights, and the drop into the glacial river below was a hundred metres or more.

Many of the wooden slats were missing and there were places where you had to leap across gaps that were frighteningly wide, using just the frayed ropes as handrails.

She didn't want to show any fear in front of Kami but he saw she was trembling and white in the face as she reached the far side.

Shortly after making the crossing the trail became steeper and more demanding. Conversation petered out as they climbed one valley wall after another. The lack of sleep began to tell; Kami felt weirdly light-headed, like he was floating a few metres above the ground.

By late morning they were travelling through a vast forest. In the middle they found a small encampment where a band of men were burning wood to create charcoal. They were rough working types covered in soot from head to toe, but they greeted these new arrivals cheerfully and offered them tea.

'Have you seen a man with a gun?' Kami asked them.

'He came past just after dawn,' one of the charcoal burners told them, 'miserable-looking character, didn't even say Namaste.'

Just after dawn! Shreeya and Kami exchanged a look of quiet satisfaction. They were definitely moving faster than their quarry and after one night on the trail were now just five or six hours behind him.

'What's your business with him?' another asked curiously.

'He's hunting for snow leopards,' Shreeya told him, sipping her sweet tea, 'and we're going to stop him.'

The men roared with laughter at this and the children's cheeks flared red with embarrassment. Kami thought they should have come up with a cover story that sounded a little more plausible, but he knew that Shreeya was incapable of lying.

'Do your parents know you're doing this?' one of them asked sharply.

'Yes,' Kami answered. He got a hard look from Shreeya for this reply, but he figured he wasn't exactly lying.

'Better you go back to your village,' the wisest looking of the men told them in a kindly tone. 'I saw that man and I wouldn't want to mess around with him.'

'We're going to Langtang anyway,' Kami said hurriedly, 'but thanks for the advice.'

The conversation died away and the children hurried to finish their drinks. They thanked the charcoal burners and hit the trail again, refreshed by the sweet tea and disturbed by these new words of warning.

'I think it's better we try and avoid talking to people,' Shreeya said.

Kami agreed with her, and from that point on they ran into the forest and hid on the rare occasions they heard people coming towards them.

On the second night fatigue began to wear them down. They had been moving for thirty hours without a significant rest and both were staggering with exhaustion. The battery in their single torch had run out and they found themselves tripping along a narrow and greasy section of the trail high above a rushing river.

'This trail is too dangerous,' Kami said finally in despair. 'We can't see enough. If we slip here … '

He didn't need to say any more. Shreeya had already had a narrow escape, managing to prevent a fall only by grabbing hold of Kami's arm.

'Let's rest for a while.'

They climbed away from the track, pushing up a slope through thick vegetation until they found a flat enough place. Shreeya pulled out the blanket and they wrapped it tight around their shoulders, grateful for the warmth it gave them on this chilled night.

'We've got the biscuits,' Shreeya mumbled, but Kami didn't have the energy to reply, let alone rummage for them in the pack.

Shreeya put her head against Kami's shoulder and he placed his arm around her. He could hear her teeth chattering for a while, but he pulled the blanket ever tighter and before long they were comfortably warm.

Lulled by the constant rushing sound of the river below, the two children soon fell into an exhausted sleep.

Strange dreams haunted them both and they woke with aching bones with the first hint of dawn.

'Come on,' Shreeya urged him as she quickly stuffed the blanket into the pack. 'We're losing time.'

They shared a packet of biscuits and a couple of handfuls of dried plums for breakfast, eating as they went along and sipping handfuls of cool water from the many springs that lined the valley walls. The morning was scorchingly hot and a thick vapour of steaming mist cloaked the giant ferns and palms.

They were moving fast and imagined they might spot the hunter on the trail ahead at any moment. Progress would have to be silent from now on, any conversation kept to whispers and nothing more.

'What are we going to do when we find him?' Kami

hissed to Shreeya as they moved swiftly along the path.

Both of them knew this was the weak spot in their plan.

'Something will turn up,' Shreeya shrugged. It was the best she could do.

The cooler hours of the afternoon came on as they reached the mountains of Langtang. In this more open terrain, they felt exposed and vulnerable. You could see for miles here and the idea that the hunter might spot them was constantly on their minds.

Finally, they reached the holy lakes, where they had a clear line of vision to the high pass that would lead across to the leopards' valley.

'Can you see him?' Kami was looking for any sign of movement on the far slopes.

'No. He's probably already gone over the col.'

They hurried round the lakes as the climb became more rugged, the trail rising across boulder slopes and sharp fields of scree.

After an hour they stopped to sip some water. Then they made an unwelcome discovery; back where they had come from three tiny figures could be seen. They were grown men, moving fast, and the two children guessed instantly who they were.

'I think that's my father,' Shreeya exclaimed in dismay,

'and two others. They're following us.'

'It had to happen. We shouldn't blame them,' Kami said, 'they're frightened for us.'

'Maybe they changed their minds,' Shreeya suggested more brightly as a new thought entered her mind. 'Perhaps they came to help us save the leopards.'

Kami shook his head.

'I don't think so,' he told her. 'They're here to stop us. Not him. If they catch up with us they'll take us back to the village.'

Kami saw that Shreeya was welling up; they were both so tired, and they had given so much already. The thought of being stopped when they were so close to the leopards' den was truly heartbreaking.

There was only one answer; keep moving. Faster than ever.

One hour later they breached the col and staggered down into the far valley – both at their physical limit. For the first time in his life, Kami began to feel that he was asking his body to do something it simply could not deliver.

Shreeya was the same, he could see, or perhaps even worse. Her feet were less hardened to this type of trek and each one was now sporting half a dozen really nasty-looking blisters.

But the knowledge that the adults were in hot pursuit gave them new determination and soon they were picking their way down the final scree slope before entering the forest.

They recognised the terrain now, limping as quickly as they could through the trees and slowing to a walking pace as they saw the glade ahead.

'Look!' Shreeya hissed with anguish.

In the centre of the meadow they now saw a small object, some sort of dead animal.

CHAPTER 4

For a horrorstruck heartbeat or two, Shreeya thought it might be one of the snow leopard cubs. Then she realised the colour of the fur was too dark, too red, and she recognised it as a juvenile deer.

'That's his plan,' Kami whispered. 'He's shot a deer and put it there as bait. He's going to wait for the leopards to come out and feed.'

'There he is!' Shreeya had spotted the hunter, creeping along the treeline directly opposite their position.

They watched as the hunter moved along the shadowy hinterland, his rifle cradled in his arms. Suspense was building. They still had no effective plan and the journey could be for nothing if even one of the cats was shot and killed.

'Oh, no!' Shreeya spotted a blur of movement. 'The cubs are out of the den. They must have smelled the carcass.'

The hunter had seen the cats too. He stepped back, melting into the shadows.

'What's he doing now?' Kami asked. His eyesight was not nearly so sharp as Shreeya's at the great distance.

'Taking something out of his sack. Something … ' Shreeya gasped. 'Kami, he's loading the gun!'

The hunter placed the sack carefully behind a tree and started to move into the meadow. He did this with great stealth and considerable skill, slipping like a shadow between boulders and bushes.

The children watched in absolute silence, a growing sensation of helplessness overwhelming them.

'What can we *do*?' Shreeya whispered.

'When we see the leopards we can scream, scare them away,' Kami suggested, his voice utterly lacking conviction.

A silence fell between them. Both knew the flaw in this plan and it was a deadly one. If they revealed themselves to the hunter by shouting or screaming to alert the leopards then he might easily shoot them on the spot.

Kami's mind was racing through the possibilities and he got to wondering what might be in the hunter's sack.

'How much ammunition has he got in that bag do

you think?'

'Plenty. He was picking out handfuls. Why? What's on your mind?'

What was on Kami's mind was something he had witnessed a few years before, when an older boy in the village had thrown a shotgun cartridge onto a fire for a laugh and almost got himself killed as the thing exploded with savage force.

If that was what could happen with a single cartridge, Kami wondered, what would the explosion be like with a few dozen?

Surely that would be enough to scare the leopards away for good?

'I'm going to sneak around, try and get his bag,' he told Shreeya. 'I can light a fire, use the cartridges, set up an explosion in the woods.'

Shreeya considered the plan, frowning as she realised how risky it was. But she could see from Kami's face that he was set on doing it.

'OK. It's a chance. But, Kami ... be careful ... please.'

Kami stepped back into the dark embrace of the forest and began to skirt slowly round the glade in a big semi-circle. He had to get behind the man's position to pick up the sack – a risky move that would take him to within fifty metres of the hunter's position.

Step by step he flanked the meadow.

The hunter had his back to him. Kami prayed to the gods he stayed that way.

Finally, he moved out of cover and stepped towards the tree where the bag was placed. It was the moment of maximum exposure. Kami was now in full view. If the hunter happened to turn around he would be seen immediately.

When he got close enough, Kami reached forward and grabbed the sack. The hunter had no idea his possessions were being stolen.

Back in the forest Kami opened up the sack and tipped the contents onto the ground. It didn't contain much, just some dried meat, a couple of wicked-looking boning knives – and about fifty shotgun cartridges.

Fifty! Kami was exultant as he saw the haul. If he got the job right he could manufacture an awesome explosion.

Kami hurried as he paced out a good distance from the enemy. He had to choose the spot carefully; far enough away that the hunter wouldn't hear him starting the fire, but not so far that the exploding cartridges would fail to have the desired effect.

At seventy steps he found a possible site. It was as good a place as any to do the job and Kami busied himself gathering twigs and sticks, choosing the dry ones which would create little smoke.

His back tingled with a dread anticipation as he worked. At any second he feared the hunter would surprise him; put a bullet through his spine.

He struck a match and blew on a handful of dried grass to nourish a flame. The burning grass licked at his hands, then flared up higher. He added kindling, threw on branches, and within minutes had a robust little fire roaring away.

He gathered up the cartridges, counting a total of fifty-two.

There was no doubt that so many cartridges would create one heck of a bang … but how long would they take to blow? One minute? Ten? Perhaps they would even explode instantaneously, not giving him enough time to get away.

He decided to chance it.

He put the all of the cartridges in the bag, threw the sack on to the fire and ran for it.

Back at the meadow, Shreeya could see that the moment of truth was approaching. The two leopard cubs were back in partial view; the dead deer had got their attention and they wanted to check the carrion out.

There! Shreeya's heart jumped a few beats as she saw the unmistakeable silhouette of the mother cat. A split second of movement between two boulders.

She saw the hunter's body stiffen with excitement. His shoulders came up a bit and he shifted the position of the gun slightly. So, he had seen the leopard too!

At that moment Shreeya saw movement next to the dead deer. A raven had circled out of the sky and landed a few metres from the body. Then a second raven flapped down and joined the first. Soon the two birds were squabbling over the body as they started to rip into it.

The snow leopards seemed irritated by the birds, Shreeya thought, but also seemed to be made bolder by their presence. Perhaps they realised the clock was ticking; they had to get a move on or their free lunch would disappear in front of their eyes.

The first of the cubs slunk out of the rocks and placed a tentative – and very large – paw on the grass. It scented the air, instincts already finely tuned even at that young age, alert for anything threatening or unusual.

The creature's coat was gorgeous. The mother cat had done a good job, had nourished her cubs with unconditional love and Shreeya's heart went into freefall at the thought of how close the leopard was to losing one or even both of her cubs.

That was the moment that something crucial clicked

inside this young Nepali girl. There was no doubt about it;
she would give her life to save these creatures, she realised,
her love for them was that strong.

It was a defining moment and it gave her great courage.

Over in the forest, some distance behind the hunter's
position, she could now see a faint tendril of smoke rising
into the sky. Kami had the fire going, she realised.

But where was the explosion?

A minute dragged past. Meanwhile, Kami snuck up as
close as he dared to the hunter and picked up a rock. In
his mind was a last ditch possibility – to try and stun the
man with a lucky throw.

*Why hadn't the cartridges blown? Had something gone
wrong?*

Shreeya knew the moment had come. The two cubs
had been provoked by the ravens and were now strutting
boldly out from cover. The hunter had a perfect line of
sight and disaster was here and now.

She couldn't wait for the explosion. Her heart thudding
like a jackhammer, she took a few steps into the glade, then
began to sprint as she called.

'Hey! HEY! Over here!'

The leopards froze in shock. Then they bolted.

Shreeya saw a look of rage flash across the man's face.

He swivelled the weapon, trying to follow the fleeing leopards, desperately looking for a clear shot at the biggest of the cats. But Shreeya put herself in the direct line of fire, screaming and yelling to urge the cats on and running across his line of vision at the crucial instant.

'Run! Run!' she shrieked.

The gun blasted, but the shot was spoiled.

The leopard family vanished into the forest, moving like the wind. The hunter roared out in fury, turning the gun now directly on Shreeya. She resisted the overwhelming urge to run, flung her arms wide and braced herself in terror for what must surely come; the ripping impact of the bullets, her chest exploding in a rage of broken flesh.

In that same instant, an explosion split the air as the cartridges finally detonated in Kami's fire. The simultaneous detonation of gunpowder was ear-splittingly loud and the trees around the fire shook as they were peppered with the shot. The hunter span around in absolute shock. To him it must have seemed a whole battalion of men were out there in the woods, shooting at him.

At that same instant a rock spun out of nowhere, striking him a glancing, and painful, blow on the shoulder.

And then the cavalry really did arrive; Shreeya's father and two other men bursting into the meadow shouting the children's names. At this the hunter ran for his sack, searching for it frantically amongst the trees where he had left it.

'Hey! Hey, you! Stop there!' Shreeya's father yelled.

But the hunter had had enough. He gave up looking for his bag and slunk away into the forest, his limping frame visible for just two or three steps before he vanished.

Shreeya ran to her father and held him tight.

At the sight of his daughter, exhausted but safe, all the fury in her father melted away. He was just happy to see her alive.

'Are you hurt?' he asked. 'He shot right at you … '

'I'm all right,' Shreeya replied.

'And the cats?'

'We saved them,' Shreeya said, simply. And she moved towards Kami and embraced him hard. When she pulled away he found his shoulder was wet with her tears.

O

From that time onward Kami and Shreeya were rarely apart. Shreeya became so much a part of Kami's world that he sometimes found it hard to think of her as a separate person.

In the evenings they would sometimes go together to bathe at the village well, Kami stripped to the waist,

Shreeya, like the other girls of the village, bathing in a Sari to protect her modesty.

It was a tranquil place; a glade filled with that mysterious green light that only a forest canopy can create. Chattering Mynah birds would come to sip at the puddles; butterflies with kingfisher wings danced in stray beams of sunlight. If no one else was around, Shreeya would ask Kami to wash her hair – his calloused fingers relishing the silky texture of the touch, the spiced Indian soap filling the air with a heady scent of sandalwood and patchouli oil.

When they were finished on those evenings when the sun stubbornly refused to die, they would go to a certain grassy terrace to dry off. Situated on a high ridge, this vantage point presented them with a view right across the Himalaya. In the foreground were wooded valleys and gorges; further away, hugging the horizon, the jagged profiles of Shishapangma, Ama Dablam, Nuptse and Everest.

Kami could name them all; his father had taught him to recognise them when he was a young boy and for some reason the knowledge had stuck.

Slowly the noises of the daytime would diminish, the hawks and eagles spiralling reluctantly out of the sky as thermals died away. Distant woodpeckers fell silent. Down in the village, the little engine at the rice mill puttered out a final few smokey revolutions and fell silent. Children chattered as they made their way home.

In this place Kami and Shreeya felt invincible. The world was, after all, literally, at their feet.

But always, as the day ended, they would have to go their separate ways, to homes which were apart.

With every passing year of his life, Kami had felt closer to Shreeya. She was a friend in a way that Laxmi, his 'bride', had never been.

The sense of injustice began to gnaw away at him. What right did others have to determine his fate? How could he build a life with a girl he hardly knew, when the one he truly loved would be living close by?

It would be a life sentence of misery.

Wild thoughts came to him in the dead of night. What if he ran away with Shreeya? He had heard stories of couples their age who had taken this desperate step. Mostly they went to India and were never heard of again. Dark tales sometimes emerged of the terrible things they had to do just to survive.

Kami felt that Shreeya would go with him if he proposed it, but in his heart he knew it would never happen. He loved his family too much, and so did she. If they ran away they would never find peace.

Then came the offer to go to Everest and Kami began to see a new possibility.

Using his earnings he might be able to break the marriage pact.

But first he would have to talk to his father.

Kami chose his moment with care, a Saturday free from work when he hoped his father would be receptive to a conversation. The formal way he phrased the request caused his father to raise an eyebrow in surprise. But he took Kami to the family room where they could talk in peace.

'I guess you want to talk about Laxmi,' his father began.

'Yes, sir, I do.'

'Well it's very simple. You've got to keep to the pact and that's the end of the story.'

'I've been having other thoughts,' Kami said hesitantly.

'Well put them out of your head. Families have been making marriage pacts like this for centuries and there's no need to change things.'

'But, sir, I don't feel happy … '

'You will feel happy. Once you have Laxmi living at your side. She's a fine girl and you are lucky to have her promise. Look at me and your mother, married by a similar pact and we've never had a bad word between us.'

It was the argument Kami had most feared, for it was

indisputably true; his mother and father were indeed happy together – living proof that a marriage pact could work.

If the circumstances were right.

But his situation was different, Kami reminded himself. The circumstances were most certainly not right. He had to tell his father the truth about Shreeya, but he knew by doing so he would be drawing the conversation in a most dangerous direction.

And how to find the words?

Kami had been raised in the traditional manner of a Nepali family. Rigid social codes dictated the way that men behaved towards women, children towards elders. Obedience to his father was absolutely at the core of who he was and he had never imagined a scenario in which he could disobey him.

But now that moment had come and Kami felt the exquisite pain of something stretching and breaking inside him as he said the next words.

'I don't want to make my life with Laxmi.'

These words provoked exactly the reaction Kami had feared. The look of fury in his father's eyes was truly terrifying. For a terrible moment he thought he would lash out with his fists.

'It's Shreeya who has put you up to this!' his father raged.

'Don't think I don't know. The whole village knows about you two.'

'It's not her.' Kami was mortified that his father was trying to twist the blame. 'This is my decision.'

'I should talk to her father. Get her sent away.'

Kami felt his guts churn as this new threat. How stupid of him not to think of it. It would be easy for his father to arrange. Get Shreeya's family to send her away to some far off place, marry her swiftly to someone else.

'You wouldn't do that.'

'Wouldn't I? It's no more than you both deserve,' his father spat the words.

'Is there no other way?' Kami asked. 'Something we can do to break the contract?'

'*Break the contract?* Who has put such thoughts in your head?'

'If we repay the dowry? Surely there is a way?'

'You don't know what you are talking about. Her family and our family have been trading for generations. There's more at stake than just this marriage.'

'But it *can* happen,' Kami insisted. 'Plenty of people have told me so. If Chandra agrees a price.'

'All right,' he conceded, finally. 'It can happen that the contract is annulled. But normally it happens because of a terrible sickness, or a death in the family, or some other tragedy.'

Kami's father put his head in his hands. He looked so close to absolute despair that for a moment Kami was almost tempted to retract everything he had said, so deeply did he want to free his father from the pain.

But something held him back.

'Tell me how you feel about this girl Shreeya,' his father said at last.

Kami looked at him directly, surprised to find that at this crucial moment, he did not feel any shame or doubt.

'I love her, sir. And I will love her for the rest of my life.'

Kami felt his father's eyes bore in to him. Such a gaze would normally make him flinch but at that moment he found he could hold the eye contact without fear, for the statement he had just made had come from his heart.

'We have to do it,' Kami implored. 'Please, father, I beg you.'

His father stood, stepping to the window and looking out across the fields of maize and rice. He sighed deeply and Kami sensed that he had reached a decision.

'I won't get involved in this. I don't agree with any of it,' his father said emphatically. 'If anyone is to try and break the contract it is up to you alone. But I warn you that Chandra is a tough man. He might throw you out of the window rather than listen to such talk.'

Kami's father cut the conversation at that point and a period of a few days followed in which Kami hardly slept at all.

Three days later Kami arrived at Laxmi's family home.

His stomach was tied in knots. It was the first time he had been to the house and he guessed it would be the last. He announced himself to Laxmi's seventeen-year-old brother and waited until her father Chandra returned from the fields.

The man greeted Kami with a courteous 'Namaste' before retreating to the yard to wash away the dust and dirt of a hard day tilling the soil. When he came back, Kami was literally shaking with fear; the moment had come and he had no idea how things would work out.

'I imagine you are here to discuss Laxmi,' Chandra said, fixing Kami with a cool gaze. 'Are you ready to take her to your home?'

A silence fell as Kami wondered how to respond. He had rehearsed these words a thousand times but now it came to the moment he felt tongue tied and lost.

'I cannot take Laxmi to my house, sir. I … I wish to make my home with another.'

The words caused an instant shift of mood. A dark

shadow swept across Chandra's face. Laxmi's father was now staring at him with ill-disguised contempt.

'I … It's something that I've thought about most seriously, sir.'

Kami wilted under his acid gaze, he saw himself as a pathetic child next to this experienced and widely respected man. What right did he have to enter his house as the bearer of such news?

It was wrong.

But not as wrong as marrying without love.

'What does your father say?' Chandra snapped.

'He says it is not my business to try and change things.'

Laxmi's father nodded.

'So why don't you listen to him? Do you not respect the wishes of your own father?'

'Yes, sir, I do. But no matter how much I love and honour him, I cannot marry Laxmi.'

'But you are *already* married to my daughter,' Laxmi's father replied indignantly. 'You speak of it as some future event but it happened many years ago and you must honour it.'

'Sir, the truth is this; my heart belongs to another.'

At that all the blood ran out of the old man's face and he looked truly desperate.

'Everything is arranged!' he hissed. 'The dowry has been paid many years ago and I cannot afford another. If you don't take her no one else will.'

'And if I repay the dowry?'

Chandra gave a bitter laugh;

'You? Who earns nothing?'

'I have work with an expedition, sir. To Everest. Earning dollars,' Kami told him.

Chandra looked unimpressed with this. 'You'll lose it playing cards and drinking beer,' he said scornfully, 'like all the young guys do.'

'No, sir. I swear I will save every last cent. All of that money will go towards paying back the dowry.'

Laxmi's father stared long and hard at Kami.

'I cannot go through with this marriage, sir,' Kami told him insistently. 'This is the only path and I swear on my life that you will be paid what you desire.'

A glimmer of resignation flickered across Chandra's face. It seemed he saw something unmoveable in Kami's expression. He sighed deeply and went to the window where he stood for a long while. When he turned back, Kami was horrified to see a tear glistening on the man's cheek.

'You will have to repay the dowry threefold,' Chandra said wearily. 'But if you fail to do so before Laxmi's sixteenth birthday then I will hold you to the marriage contract and you will take her to your house.'

'Thank you, sir.' Kami bowed deeply to Chandra and walked down the stairs in a daze. As he left the house he heard the sound of wailing from an upstairs window.

Laxmi had been told.

He could not feel sorry for her. If he could pay back the dowry and the extra sum her father had demanded, she would be free to marry again. And maybe she would find someone who would really love her.

Surely like that her life would be more complete?

As he walked back to his village Kami thought about the figure that Laxmi's father had mentioned.

Three times the dowry.

It was an enormous sum. Even the briefest mental calculation revealed how hopeless the situation really was. Kami had mentioned the dollars he would earn on the Everest expedition but the reality was that he would have to work on two or three such trips to save such a fortune.

It was an overwhelming thought and it left Kami with no peace of mind.

Luckily, at that time, the Everest expedition was approaching fast and Jamling invited him to attend a climbing camp he had organised on one of the Khumbu's many glaciers.

Kami was jubilant; the ten-day course was a final chance to practise his climbing techniques. He worked hard, perfecting the skills he would need on the great peak and proving himself to be a natural at ice climbing and rope work.

When he got back home – with four weeks to go to the expedition – he continued his physical training, loading up his rucksack with two huge slabs of slate and yomping up and down the steepest slope he could find until he was panting with exhaustion.

He hoped it would be enough; he knew that Everest Sherpas were famed throughout the world for their speed, strength and endurance. Jamling was taking a gamble to bring him along on the expedition and he wanted to make him proud.

Late at night, working by hurricane lantern with Shreeya at his side, he would practise his English. Jamling's advice on this had also struck home; he knew that he would never be allowed to go high on the mountain if he couldn't communicate properly with the clients.

Shreeya was a hard taskmaster but a good teacher; eight years of schooling had given her almost perfect English and she was quick to pick Kami up on his errors.

Shortly before Kami left, Shreeya fixed a surprise; the local school owned several small digital cameras and Shreeya had arranged for one to be loaned to Kami for the Everest expedition. One of the teachers quickly taught him how to use it.

Shreeya looked on proudly, but also with regret. She knew that the time of parting was nearly upon them.

Finally, the moment came. Kami packed his few belongings in a tatty old canvas rucksack and waited in the yard of the house for the family to gather.

His father held him by the shoulders, 'You have a great opportunity,' he said. 'The first of our family to have the honour to go to Sagarmatha.'

Kami nodded. He felt tears welling up and didn't trust himself to speak. His mother took his hand and squeezed it, a rare show of affection.

'Make us proud, Kami,' she said.

'I will try,' Kami promised.

Then he strapped on his pack and turned to go, walking away from the village of his birth, heading for the trails which would lead ever upwards to the village of Lukla and the rendezvous with the expedition.

A short time later an elegant figure slipped from the shadows of a field of tall maize and joined him on the track. It was Shreeya, come to accompany him for the first stage of the journey.

They walked side by side, through terraced valleys where tender shoots of rice were sprouting in the spring sunshine. The world was coming alive after the frigid embrace of winter and great flights of snowcocks were flying in from the south.

The further they got from the village the more the heavy shroud of responsibility seemed to lift. Trekking through unknown villages, they felt free, invisible even. For that one day it was as if Laxmi and the marriage pact did not exist at all.

Neither of them really wanted to stop. It felt like they could just keep walking forever.

Kami begged Shreeya to return before she was missed but she insisted on spending one last night together. They built a fire in the forest and baked wild apples in the coals. Later, wrapped in Kami's coarse blanket, their body heat keeping out the chill night air, they held each closer than they had ever done before.

They parted the following morning, on a high col where wild flowers filled the air with perfume. That was when Shreeya gave Kami her parting gift; the little bronze shrine bell that had been a part of her family home for so many years.

'This was given to me as a birth present,' she told him shyly. 'Place it on the summit, if the gods will allow.'

Greatly moved, Kami held the little bell in his hands, already aware of the enormity of the gesture. Placing this devotion in the home of the gods would be the ultimate holy act.

A tribute from both of them and a symbol of hope for the future.

If he could do it.

CHAPTER 5

Kami reached Lukla on the third day of his trek. Normally he was here with his father, an outsider come to trade, and he had always loved the bustle and colour of this busy market town. This time he was here on his own, with a certain strut to his stride – he was here to be a part of an Everest *expedition*.

He was bursting with pride.

He asked around for Jamling and was directed to a certain guest house in the high part of town.

'You're bang on time,' Jamling told him, 'the work's just beginning!'

He guided Kami to a small field where the expedition was readying itself for departure. Kami had never seen such an incredible mess in his life – it looked like a hurricane had ripped through a refugee camp. There were scattered piles of yak fodder, teetering towers of tinned food and, spread out in the sun, just about every variety of tent known to man.

And rope; everywhere, rope! Rope hanging from the trees. Rope drying on the walls. Red rope. Yellow rope. New rope. Old rope. Thousands upon thousands of metres of rope.

As for the Sherpa team, they paid Kami little attention, but didn't seem surprised to have him around. They chatted quietly between themselves as they worked, catching up with news after weeks or months of rest since their last expedition.

'You have to meet the Sirdar,' Jamling told him, 'his name's Tenzing – named after the first Sherpa to climb the great mountain. Seven times Everest summit.'

Seven times to the summit of Everest! Kami wondered at the superhuman powers such a man must have.

They tracked Tenzing down in a local store, where he was bargaining for sacks of flour. He was younger than Kami had imagined, perhaps only thirty, but his eyes were those of an older and more experienced man.

His nose was oddly shaped, the tip missing and the surrounding tissue puckered with scar tissue. It gave him a grizzled look, rather scary, and Kami wondered if it was another form of frostbite injury.

'This is the lad I told you about,' Jamling told him.

The Sirdar gave Kami an appraising look, slapping him hard on the back and pinching the lad's bicep in a vice like grip.

'Good enough,' Tenzing nodded. 'Take these sacks of flour back to the base.'

The two men left Kami to the job, a simple task which left him with his face and hair covered with white flour.

Then he was told to report to Lopsang, the 'second Sirdar' and Kami's direct boss. He was a slightly chubby man, with a deadpan expression and a twinkle in his eye. Unlike Tenzing, he had never summitted Everest, but had vast experience as a quartermaster and the type of logistical mind needed to keep an expedition fed, housed and watered for three long months.

'You need to check all these tents,' he told Kami. 'Put them up. Check the seams. Repair the holes. Count the pegs.'

He showed Kami an impressive pile of tents.

'If there's anything you can't repair, let me know,' he said, as he moved off to attend to other matters.

Kami found a vacant scrap of ground and emptied the contents of one of the stuff sacks out. A bewildering stash of gear fell at his feet.

Kami had put up tents on his previous expeditions but these looked different.

Luckily, Nima, one of the other Sherpa lads, came over to help Kami out.

'Let me give you a hand,' he said good-naturedly. 'You obviously don't know your ass from your elbow.'

Nima showed him how to assemble the carbon fibre poles and thread them through the correct guides in the fabric.

'Quite easy,' Kami observed.

'Wait 'til you try that in a force-ten storm at eight thousand metres,' Nima laughed. 'Then you'll see if it's easy or not.'

'Have you been to Everest before?' Kami asked him shyly.

'Twice. Once to the summit last year,' Nima told him with considerable pride and, with that, left Kami mulling over his response.

Twice to Everest! And Nima really didn't look much older than seventeen. Kami felt intensely jealous of such a wealth of experience, but he had liked Nima and he reckoned they would become friends.

The work went on. Many of the tents were veterans of previous expeditions and there was plenty of damage to repair with special glue. A surly looking lad called Pemba was ordered to work with Kami, but Kami didn't like him much; all he seemed to do was boast about all the girlfriends he had.

As they worked, Kami noticed that a number of youths were hanging around outside the compound walls. They were strong looking boys, fifteen or sixteen years old, and they were eager to strike up a conversation with anyone working in the compound.

'Those lads are looking for work,' Lopsang told him when he came to inspect the progress. 'Some of them wait for years before they get a break. Some never get a break at all.'

Kami eyed the gathered boys, wondering, not for the first time, at his luck. Why was he the one that had been favoured by the gods? Why was it him who had the job with the expedition? Was it a reward for his years of prayer? Or just down to chance?

Maybe the answer would come during the expedition, he thought. A pleasing idea.

Gradually Kami and Pemba worked their way through the pile of tents. By nightfall their fingers were cramped up and their eyes were red and raw from the fumes.

'You sniffed so much glue today you probably flew over the summit,' Lopsang laughed. 'Come and get some supper, you've earned it.'

Kami was grateful for the break and he wolfed down the rice and sauce, watching the vast piles of equipment as they were gradually sorted and packed into barrels.

As the most junior member of the team, Kami wasn't entitled to a tent of his own. Instead he was given a sleeping bag and told to bunk down in the mess tent. He wasn't alone; five or six of the other younger Sherpas had the same quarters.

It was hard to relax. The tent was fuggy with cigarette smoke and a few of the Sherpas were sitting at the table drinking chang and playing cards.

The bag smelled a bit sweaty but it was warm. Lulled by the gentle chatter of the men, Kami finally felt himself slipping into a deep and dreamless sleep.

O

The kerosene cooker flared into life just before 6 a.m. Kami stumbled out into a misty dawn and went to wash. He had to break a thin glaze of ice that had formed on the washing bowl but the bitingly cold water was deliciously fresh on his skin.

Back in the tent, handfuls of cheap black Indian tea were thrown into boiling water. Kami was given a chipped tin mug of it and he added a couple of spoonfuls of sugar for good measure.

Just after 8 a.m. a throaty siren blasted off down at the airstrip.

'That's the boss flying in!' Tenzing announced.

Kami and Nima bolted down the last of their breakfast chapattis and followed the Sirdar down to the runway. As they approached, the hornet buzz of an incoming aircraft was echoing around the walls of the valley.

Kami had seen aeroplanes passing overhead in his village but never at close hand. The shiny green and white turbo prop that finally bounced onto the runway seemed to him more like a toy than anything, dwarfed as it was by the stupendous snow-dusted walls that surrounded the town.

A film crew exited the aircraft, scurrying towards the front of the plane to frame up a shot before yelling back.

'OK. We're rolling.'

That was the cue for Alex Brennan to make his entrance, stepping confidently from the cabin of the little plane and moving swiftly to shake hands with a row of local dignitaries who had turned out to greet him.

'That's the boss,' Tenzing said to Kami.

Kami was impressed by his first view of Alex Brennan; he was a physically imposing figure already dressed for the high mountains.

'Hi guys.' Brennan shook hands with each of the waiting

Sherpas. 'Good to see you all.'

Other Westerners were brought over to meet the Sherpa team; the two-man film crew, a pretty female journalist called Sasha, and a couple of burly, unsmiling characters who were introduced only as 'friends' of the boss.

It should have taken five minutes to walk from the airfield to the town, but in fact it took almost an hour. News of Alex Brennan's arrival had spread like wildfire and a whole bunch of trekkers, for the most part American, were keen to shake his hand and have a photo taken with the great man.

'A pleasure to meet you, ma'am. Thank you for your kind words. A pleasure to meet you, sir … ' And so it went on, with well-wishers from Texas, from Illinois, from Montana and Oregon.

Brennan was the personification of charm, pressing the flesh with practised ease and seeming to have time for everyone. Kami sensed that there was a genuine excitement in the air; these people really *liked* Alex Brennan, they *believed* in him, trusted him.

'Why does he need to come to Everest?' Kami whispered to Tenzing. He seemed to be a man who already had everything.

'Publicity!' Tenzing exclaimed with a laugh. 'Perhaps he wants to be even more famous.'

There was only one slightly strange thing that Kami noticed – the two burly Americans who had arrived with Brennan on the aircraft were hovering right next to him as he met the trekkers.

'Bodyguards,' Pemba suggested with a tingle of excitement. 'Maybe they have guns.'

'Why?' Kami questioned. 'What are they afraid of?'

'I don't know, terrorists, assassins, kidnappers.'

'But why would anyone want to hurt him?'

'Think about it,' Tenzing replied. 'He's rich, he's famous all over America, maybe one day he'll even be the president. There are plenty of crazy people who would like to kill someone like that.'

'But not in Nepal.' Kami could not imagine that any Nepali would ever seek to harm someone like Alex Brennan.

'No. But they can't take any chances.'

Finally, they made it to the field where the expedition convoy was preparing for departure. Yaks were loaded up and one hour later they were all set.

The expedition filed out of Lukla as the trek to Base Camp began.

O

The first couple of hours went smoothly, the Westerners leading on, chatting excitedly and snapping away on their cameras, and the Sherpas and pack animals following behind. In addition to the load on his back, Kami was in charge of three of the heavily laden yaks, urging them forward with a mixture of guttural cries and the occasional well-aimed rock.

The film crew were shooting almost constantly, framing up shots at scenic turns of the trail and firing questions spontaneously at the Sherpas when the mood took them.

Kami found George the cameraman walking alongside him with the camera running.

'How does it feel to have so much weight on your back?' George asked.

'Not so bad. I do it every day,' Kami replied with a smile.

The truth was that Kami had little energy to waste on conversation. He was carrying two kit bags, a total weight of almost forty kilos, and his legs were feeling it with every step.

A couple of hours from Lukla the expedition passed through a small village which had suffered a recent tragedy: a landslide had ripped out a large chunk of hillside, sweeping houses and fields away in an avalanche of boulders, mud and splintered trees.

'I want some shots of this,' Alex Brennan told the camera team. 'This is the reality of life in the Himalaya.'

Brennan led the camera crew up the slope, filming as they went while he gave a running commentary on the devastation.

'This is the remains of someone's house. You can see clothes and other personal stuff in the wreckage here. I can see a doll. A broken cot. I shudder to think how many people must have died in this landslide.'

Kami and a few of the other Sherpas followed on reluctantly, carrying the film crew's spare flight cases and an extra tripod. The air smelled bacterial, of musty churned earth and crushed bark with, here and there, the unmistakeable stench of decomposition.

'We shouldn't be here,' Tenzing muttered. 'Disturbing the spirits.'

Kami nodded his agreement.

Further up the scarred section of mountain they came across a lone man toiling amidst the debris. Filthy from head to foot, he was evidently bone tired, pulling broken roof beams from the debris field.

'This is incredible,' Brennan said to camera, 'this man is actually rebuilding his house with his own bare hands. That just tells you everything you need to know about the spirit of the Sherpa people.'

Faced with this unexpected invasion, the man just stared at them all with a bewildered look on his face. Kami felt very sorry for him.

'We're going to help this guy out,' Brennan said suddenly. 'I want you Sherpas to give me a hand.'

So saying, Alex Brennan stripped off to the waist and began hauling rocks onto the platform. The Sherpas just stood there, part ashamed by this unexpected display of human flesh, and part dumbstruck to see that Alex Brennan owned a torso that wouldn't have looked out of place in a bodybuilders' convention.

'What's wrong guys?' Sasha teased them. 'You never seen an *American* before?'

'Come on dudes,' Brennan urged them. 'Think of it as a team-building exercise.'

'You heard the man,' Sasha smiled at the Sherpas, 'I guess it's time to get our hands dirty.'

Kami and the other Sherpas bent themselves to the task, roaming down the slope from the site of the destroyed house and extracting what they could. Sasha worked gamely alongside them, snatching big stones to her belly and staggering up the slope to the building site.

'I'm not paid to do this,' Pemba grumbled. It seemed to

Kami that he never stopped complaining.

The film crew stuck to Alex Brennan like glue, shadowing him as he darted about the debris field, his torso glistening as it trickled with mud and sweat.

'I think this is what foreigners call a 'photo opportunity,' Tenzing told Kami.

Brennan had a phenomenal work rate. He consistently chose the biggest boulders to shift and the heaviest timbers to pull from the slime.

But, finally, he met his match.

A huge great roof beam, buried deep in the debris field with just a short length protruding.

Brennan braced his feet against bedrock and seized the timber. His hands were so huge they virtually encircled the whole beam. He took a deep breath and pulled back hard.

No movement. It didn't budge a single inch.

Brennan's brow crinkled at that. A quizzical look swept across his face, as if he was tasting an unfamiliar food.

'You need some help there?' Sasha asked him with a smile.

'No, no. I'm on it.'

He tried again but the stubborn shaft of wood was staying put. After much puffing and grunting Brennan gave up on the buried beam and turned to the camera with a shrug and a wry smile.

'I guess there's always one that gets away.'

The camera crew moved in closer to Brennan at that point and began an interview with him.

Kami listened for a few moments as the American chatted, then he got to thinking about that beam. He eyed it up closely, thinking that it didn't really look so much bigger than the ones he hauled about the hillsides with his father.

He straddled the rafter and gripped it hard. He bent his legs down and sucked air into his lungs. Then with one smooth upward movement he plucked the beam out of the ground with a great sucking sound of wet mud.

He let one end of the beam rest on the ground for a second or two while he caught his breath, then he dropped his right arm and let the beam nestle right across his shoulders.

And only then did he realise that everyone around him had gone silent.

Kami stopped and turned. The camera was pointing right at him.

'Holy crap!' Brennan exclaimed. He turned to the crew. 'Did you *get* that?'

'Yep.'

Kami quickly turned, resuming the climb, regretting already that he had drawn attention to himself. He hoped they would stop filming him, but no such luck. A few seconds later Brennan and the crew were hurrying after him.

'That was a pretty awesome piece of work. What's your name, son?'

Kami felt a hot flush of embarrassment engulf him.

'Kami, sir.'

Kami reached the platform where he let the beam fall onto the pile along with the other timbers.

'Kami, did you say?' Brennan slapped the young Sherpa hard on the back and then placed his arm around him to twist him towards the camera.

'Ladies and gentlemen,' he said grandly, 'I give you Kami Sherpa. Boy of steel. No, let's make that tungsten!'

The expedition left the landslide site and picked up the trail towards Phakding. The unexpected work session had broken the ice between the Westerners and the Sherpas, and Kami found himself trekking next to Sasha.

'That was pretty funny what happened back there,' she said.

'I didn't mean it to be like that,' Kami blurted out. 'I was just trying to help.'

Sasha placed a hand gently on his shoulder.

'Hey, I didn't mean people were laughing *at* you.'

'OK.' Kami kept his head down.

'Alex didn't mind, you know. He was laughing along with everyone else.'

'I hope so.'

They reached a small suspension bridge over a canyon where the team were forced to walk in single file. Kami took the opportunity to pick up his pace, getting sufficiently far ahead of Sasha that the conversation had to stop.

He felt bad to cut her off like that but he really wasn't in the mood to talk.

He felt bad about the incident back at the landslide. All his life, Kami had always hated being the focus of attention.

And it must have seemed like he was showing off in front of the boss.

He thought about Shreeya to distract himself, focusing on where she would be at this time of day. Perhaps weaving a blanket with her aunt. Maybe cutting grass for the buffalo or the goats. He wondered if she was thinking about him. And gradually he began to feel a bit better.

At the small riverside village of Phakding the team eased off their loads and pitched camp on a dusty field. In less than half an hour the tents were pitched, kit bags were distributed to their rightful owners and the kerosene stoves were roaring as the first kettles of boiling water began to sing.

Later, Kurt set up his satellite dish and connected up his laptop so that he could access the internet.

'The satellite weather prediction is saying rain,' he told the gathered Sherpas.

Kami was amazed. It seemed pretty staggering that Kurt's laptop could connect to a satellite up there in space, and that pictures of swirling weather systems could be viewed with just a few clicks of a mouse.

'That doesn't help much,' Nima grunted quietly to Kami, 'it's legpower that gets you to the top of Everest, not computers.'

Alex Brennan took his turn at the laptop and started to browse through a selection of news sites. He skipped the main headlines, concentrating – as far as Kami could see – on articles that were about his own expedition.

'Pictures of himself … ' Nima whispered to Kami with a wicked giggle. 'That's all he's interested in. Me, me, me and more me!'

Brennan suddenly whipped round and fixed Nima with a beady glare.

'What was what?' he asked sternly.

'N-n-n-nothing sir,' Nima stuttered, his face reddening fast.

Kami dragged Nima away and they beat a retreat back to

the Sherpa tent.

'You and your big mouth,' Kami admonished him.

○

Kurt's weather prediction turned out to be right and the expedition left the following morning on an overcast and drizzly day. Once again, Kami was placed in charge of three pack animals, lumbering yaks that were carrying towering loads.

At the northernmost end of Monjo village the expedition had its permits checked at the National Park headquarters.

Next to the ticket office was a small museum devoted to the culture and ecology of the Everest region. Half of the floor space was occupied by a huge plaster model of the Himalaya and the team gathered round it, quickly identifying Everest, Shishapangma and Cho Oyu.

Alex Brennan noticed how closely Kami was studying the model.

'Have you climbed any of these?' he asked Kami.

'No sir. Not yet.'

'Not yet!' Brennan laughed. 'I like that. That's the spirit.'

As the team left the park headquarters, the sky turned even more threatening and a full-blooded storm kicked off. The Westerners had their rain gear in their small daypacks and were able to Gore-Tex up and keep dry. Most of the Sherpas on the other hand, Kami included, were carrying climbing hardware and expedition food on their backs and had none of their personal gear with them.

The Sherpas got soaked to the skin as the shower turned to sheeting rain.

They crossed the river several times as the track meandered up the valley, the river seemingly more swollen from the downpour each time. A sharp, stinging wind came down from the ice-laden peaks to the north. Sleet began to slant down, followed by a brief blitz of hailstones.

Then came the notorious climb up to Namche Bazaar, a two-and-a-half-hour slog which had a justifiably ugly reputation amongst Everest trekkers. Kami was cold but he could deal with that, in fact, from his point of view everything would have been fine on this ever-rising track if only the yaks would have kept moving.

'Haaaaargh! Haaarrgh!'

Kami became quite hoarse with the constant yelling. He aimed bigger and bigger stones at the beasts' rumps but they grew surly, stubbornly refusing to budge, staring at him balefully and seeming oblivious to the stinging pain.

Then came the final push up a series of steps. Twenty minutes of stop-start progress. Finally, came the smell of wood smoke filtering through the trees and the expedition saw the spectacular natural amphitheatre around which the remarkable town of Namche Bazaar was built.

'That wasn't so bad,' Kurt said.

Kami disagreed. The constant goading of the yaks had left him exhausted and he was totally drenched. He was grateful that the acclimatisation programme insisted on a forty-eight-hour stop here to let those who had recently flown into Lukla adjust to the thin air.

'Three thousand five hundred metres,' Alex Brennan exclaimed at the mess table that night, 'only five thousand four hundred to go.'

The comment got some laughs from those at the table but it was followed by an awkward silence. Kami could see that they were all feeling the altitude here at Namche, George the cameraman had complained of a pounding headache and Sasha was looking pale and washed out.

'We have a photocall tomorrow morning,' Kurt told them, 'so we need everyone looking their best. I want the whole team up at the military post at 6 a.m.'

The press pack arrived that night: a dozen photographers, all men, representing various press agencies and newspapers in the USA, Europe and Asia.

The Sherpas were amused by the new arrivals. These

characters didn't look like trekkers and they certainly didn't behave like them. Laden down with camera bags, they wheezed and spluttered into town, dragging themselves to their lodge with cries of relief and calls for whisky and lager.

'Snappers like this spend their lives following politicians and sportsmen around,' Sasha told Kami and Nima. 'Most of their photocalls are on private jets. This might be a little out of their comfort zone.'

The lodge was overwhelmed by this marauding horde, the kitchens deluged with requests for pizzas, cheeseburgers and yak steaks, most of which went uneaten when the guests discovered just how little they resembled the familiar comfort food of home.

But the beer evidently did taste sufficiently familiar, and so did the Scotch. Kami, Pemba and Nima were loaned to the lodge owner by Tenzing and spent the entire evening acting as waiters, trying to keep up with the orders from this hard-drinking crew.

Most of the photographers paid them little notice, with one exception: a huge guy with the reddest nose Kami had ever seen who called them over to the corner where he was drinking with a buddy.

'Hey! You guys are going up there with Brennan, right?'

'Yes, sir.'

Kami thought he resembled one of the frogs that infested the fields back home. The frog man swigged deeply from his bottle of Everest beer.

'Take a seat. Let's have a little talk about stuff.'

His drinking partner gave him a dirty look. 'Leave them alone,' he said accusingly. 'They don't want to get involved in your grubby world.'

Then he left, weaving an uncertain path across the dining room.

'Don't take any notice of him,' the frog man said with a sly laugh, 'I'm not hustling you guys. I just wanted to ask you how things are going with Alex Brennan.'

The three Sherpa lads exchanged a glance. The question seemed innocent enough.

'Things are going very well, sir,' Nima replied earnestly. 'He's a great boss.'

'How about that journalist, Sasha? She fitting in OK?'

'No problems, sir,' Kami told him. 'A nice person.'

'That's great. That's all good news.'

He drank again and poured some of the beer into a glass which he offered to them. Kami declined but Nima and Pemba took an enthusiastic swig.

'You think those two are an *item*?' he asked, his eyes twinkling with mischief as he winked lecherously at them.

'You know what I mean by that, right? Maybe you've seen them sharing a tent in the night?'

The three Sherpas looked at him in surprise. The question seemed bizarre to them. Kami felt the first stirrings of alarm. This character didn't inspire much confidence.

'No sir,' he said firmly. 'Nothing like that.'

'You see Alex Brennan is engaged to a lovely lady back home. She's rich and famous like him so people like to read about them in the newspapers. That's why if there was a photo, for example, of that journalist Sasha coming out of Alex's tent one morning then it might be worth a lot of money to you guys.'

Pemba's expression brightened at the mention of cash.

'How much money?' he asked.

Kami didn't like the way the conversation was going and he kicked Pemba beneath the table to warn him to shut up. But Pemba just glared at him and kicked back harder.

'A couple of hundred dollars, maybe more,' the frog man said. 'But there would have to be a photo, you understand? The two of them together doing something … intimate.'

Pemba whistled happily at the sound of all that cash. Nima gave an eager nod, downed the rest of his beer as Kami glared at him.

'Have you got a camera?' the man asked.

'Kami's got one,' Nima said.

'Great.'

The frog man reached into his pocket, extracting a wallet from which he pulled some business cards.

'Here's my contact details. You guys know how to use email, right?'

'Yes, sir,' Pemba replied eagerly. 'There are internet cafes in almost all the villages now.'

'Great. OK, so I'll look forward to hearing from you if you see anything like that.'

Kami didn't want to offend the man so – along with the other two – he put the card in the pocket of his fleece and left him to his beer.

Back in the kitchen Kami rounded on the other two. 'You shouldn't get involved with that guy,' he told them sharply.

'Why not?' Nima shrugged. 'Money is money, right?'

'Can't you see he's stirring things up? He's a troublemaker.'

Pemba turned on Kami. 'So what? All he needs is one stupid photo. If we can make some honest money out of it then who cares?'

'But it's not honest money,' Kami insisted, 'the boss is the boss. You'd be betraying him.'

'Anyway, maybe nothing's going to happen,' Nima said sulkily. 'The boss will keep his hands off that girl and that'll be the end of it.'

'Just forget about it,' Kami told them.

Back in the Sherpa tent, Kami found sleep was elusive. The row with Nima and Pemba had been upsetting and he was angry with Nima for siding against him.

When he did manage to slip away he was plagued by unsettling dreams.

The next day turned into something of a fiasco. The late-night party had left the press guys groggy and their faces were a picture when they realised there was a brisk thirty-minute climb up a steep hill to the place where the photocall was to happen.

Tenzing ordered Kami and Nima to take a dozen chairs up the hill. They split the load between them, and, carrying six chairs each on their backs, set off with the photographers.

The walk was an eventful one. Two of the photographers vomited up their breakfast as they struggled up the slope and another had to scamper behind a bush, victim of an acute attack of diarrhoea.

Kami and Nima couldn't help sniggering at his plight and their shared laughter broke the ice between them. The argument of the previous evening seemed to be forgotten.

The place for the photocall was well chosen, an open

field with an unrestricted view of Everest and Lhotse. The location was right next to Namche's military post and a handful of chilly-looking soldiers came out of their guard posts to watch the show.

'Where's the star?' one of the photographers asked.

Kurt made a brief walkie talkie call and Alex Brennan sauntered out from one of the military buildings in the company of the base commander. Kami was struck by the theatre of the moment, it was an *entrance* in the true sense of the word and the gathered press men hurriedly picked up their cameras to get their first shots of the senator.

'Really appreciate you guys making it,' he told them. 'Now let's make sure you get what you need.'

A row of chairs was set up and the Western team members seated with Alex Brennan in the middle. The Sherpas were arranged standing up behind them and the photo session began with a blizzard of flashes as the press pack got to work.

'This way Alex!'

'Over here Alex!'

'We're going to be famous,' Nima whispered to Kami.

They smiled their way through the session and then stood aside with the rest as the press pack requested shots of Alex on his own.

'A bit to the right, Alex. We need Everest right behind you.'

'Look towards the mountain please.'

Brennan did as he was asked, smiling gracefully throughout, and then nodding almost imperceptibly to Kurt to signify he'd had enough.

'OK,' Kurt said abruptly. 'That's all, folks.'

And with that Alex Brennan beat an elegant retreat, whisked back to the camp by Kurt while the photographers compared shots on their digital screens.

The press pack spent the rest of the morning emailing their shots back to Base, then the entire circus packed up and headed for Lukla. They left behind an Everest-sized pile of empty beer bottles in the backyard of the lodge and a lingering scent of cigar smoke.

Namche suddenly seemed an empty and rather silent place.

'We pull out tomorrow,' Tenzing told the team that afternoon. 'The yaks will be here at dawn. I want the loads roped up and ready by 5 a.m.'

CHAPTER 6

Just after daybreak the team hit the trail, gaining the ridgeline in record time as the town of Namche fell rapidly away behind them. They passed through the village of Khumjung and began a spectacular traverse around a monumental cliff.

Midway through the trek Kami saw that Sasha was right behind him. Nima had told him that the Western team members would tend to group together on the trekking days so he was surprised and pleased to have her company.

He waited for her to catch up, admiring her easy grace as she picked a route along the rocky path. She had tied her blonde hair back in a pony tail and he noticed how the flowing part of it caught the sun as she approached.

'Hey Mr Tungsten!' she said cheerily. 'How's life?'

'Not bad,' Kami replied shyly.

They started to walk together. He had to pick up his speed to match her, her long legs giving her a slight pace advantage over him.

'I couldn't sleep last night I was so excited,' she told him. 'I've wanted to get to Base Camp ever since I was a little girl.'

'Really?' Kami was charmed by this.

'Yeah. This is the best reporting job I've ever had.'

'Me too. My best job,' Kami replied.

'Have you done other things?'

'Mostly cutting wood with my father.'

Sasha playfully tweaked Kami's bicep with her fingers.

'That's where you got the muscles, right?'

'I guess.'

They walked side by side for another hour as the trail entered the confines of a vast pine forest, then sat down to take some time out. Kami was packing a huge load on his back and he was relieved to get a sit down.

'So is there a little Mrs Kami waiting for you back home? I heard you guys get married really young.'

Kami laughed nervously. The comment had been a bit close to the mark.

'I don't know,' he told her. 'Maybe there's someone.'

'There you go! I *knew* you'd have some lovely Sherpani girlfriend. What's her name? Is she pretty?'

But Kami wouldn't go further. Apart from anything else, he was superstitious about uttering Shreeya's name. So he just grinned and bluffed it out.

'I'm single at the moment,' Sasha told him. 'I finished with this guy I was with back in the States. We were together for years and it all went a bit wrong at the end so I was kind of down for a while.'

Kami didn't know what to say so he just replied 'uh-huh.'

'That's why I chose this assignment,' she continued. 'It's totally simple and clean. A guy goes to Everest and climbs it. That's the type of story I need right now in my life.'

Their rest stop was over; Kami shouldered his load once more and they regained the trail as it continued to traverse the side of the massive valley.

Finally, the track reached a fork in the river and began to climb. Conversation between them petered out as the long ascent to Tengboche Monastery began to take its toll and it was late afternoon by the time they reached the high plateau.

'Phew! That was a tough one!' Sasha exclaimed as they came to a halt outside the monastery. She wrapped her arms around Kami and hugged him hard. He could smell the perfumed scent of sun tan cream on her neck.

'Come on Kami! Hug me back man! That's how we do it, you know? Don't be so … Asian!'

He held her tight for a second or two then waited until she released him.

The rest of the team soon arrived and Kami was quickly ordered to start putting up tents. As he worked he thought about that day's trek with Sasha; the conversation with her had been fun but her final comment had stung him in a curious way.

Don't be so … Asian.

Kami had never really thought of himself as Asian. Or as anything really other than just himself. But the more time he was spending with the Westerners it was true that he felt different. They were so open, so direct, so *confident* with everything.

'They are like us. And not like us,' Jamling had warned him.

Kami was beginning to see the truth of those words.

That night, in the small hours of the morning, Kami went outside to take a pee. The yaks shifted nervously at the torchlight, their coats already dusted with a layer of frost.

The night was gloriously clear. By the faint illumination of the stars he could see the delicate white/blue profile of Everest and Lhotse, still many days' walk to the north.

Over in the monastery he could hear the monks gathering for their nightly prayers. Smoke drifted across the plateau, laced with the pleasing aroma of incense.

He went back to the tent and pulled the blankets tight, shivering with cold for a few minutes before his body warmed. In the time it took him to fall asleep the monks had begun their prayers in earnest, the muffled drone of the trumpets and the clash of cymbals echoing around the village.

○

At first, the trail from Tengboche descended. As so often seemed to be the case, the route was striking against the grain of the land, forging across valleys the hard way.

They passed a number of holy shrines. Everywhere there were signs of Buddhist devotion, prayer flags strung across the rugged hillsides, scriptures carved into boulders, and prayer wheels mounted on posts outside the tea houses that cropped up along the way.

Just past the village of Pangboche the team arrived at the designated lunch spot – a field next to the river. Lopsang and his assistants had already put up trestle tables on which sandwiches and cakes were laid out ready.

The day was exceptionally warm; the spring sun blasting out of a cloudless sky. The whole team lay around sunbathing after lunch, enjoying the chance to relax. Then Sasha came back from the river and made an announcement.

'There's a bunch of kids messing around in a pool down there,' Sasha told the group. 'Anyone else fancy a swim?'

'Great idea,' Kurt replied, and within five minutes the Westerners had dug their swimming costumes out of their packs and were heading down to the riverside.

Kami followed them and put his hand in the water.

'Too cold for you?' Sasha asked him.

'I don't want to get frostbite,' he told her with a smile.

The glacial temperature didn't seem to bother the Westerners. Kami watched them for a while as they joined the local kids who had excavated the pool. There was a huge boulder above it and they all took it in turns to jump off the top, screaming and fooling about.

Then he felt Tenzing's hand on his shoulder. 'Time to do the washing up.'

The two of them returned to the kitchen tent and Kami set to work as Tenzing looked around the field.

'Where's Nima and Pemba?' the Sirdar asked him testily. 'They should be doing this with you.'

'No idea,' Kami told him.

Only later did Kami find the other two; they were huddled together in a quiet spot in the village, chatting animatedly together and staring at something that Pemba was holding.

'What are you looking at?' Kami asked them.

Pemba swiftly tucked the object into his pocket.

'Nothing,' he said.

Nima looked seriously guilty.

'Let me take a look,' Kami insisted.

'No.' Pemba stood and strutted off.

'What was it?' Kami asked Nima. But his friend made no reply. The bizarre encounter gave Kami a bad feeling and when he returned to the field he decided, on a hunch, to check his daypack where he straight away made an unwelcome discovery.

'You took my camera,' he snapped at Nima.

'It … it was a joke,' Nima blustered. But he looked gutted to have been caught.

'What were you doing with it?' Kami raged.

Nima just hung his head and mumbled an incoherent reply as the others looked on curiously.

'Tell Pemba I want it back,' Kami hissed.

The ugly little incident blotted Kami's day and he could take no enjoyment in the remaining hours of trekking as the trail rose in a series of rocky turns to a massive rocky plateau.

He kept an eye out for Pemba but he was nowhere to be seen and just before nightfall they made it to Dingboche, the last village of any size on the great trek to Base Camp.

Pemba finally showed up later that evening and he tossed the camera to Kami without a word of apology and watched with a sly smile as Kami turned it on to check it.

'Where's the memory card?' Kami demanded.

'You'll get it back later,' Pemba said. And with that he walked out.

Kami had to bite his lip. Alex Brennan and some of the other Westerners were close by and he didn't want to create a scene in front of them.

But Pemba was seriously starting to get on his nerves.

O

After supper a lively session of cards kicked off. Brennan had decided to teach some of the Sherpas poker and they had quickly taken to the game, playing each evening for a handful of rupees. That night the games got rowdy, finally climaxing with an arm wrestling competition in which Alex Brennan took on all comers.

Brennan got a big cheer from the Sherpas as he stripped to the waist.

'Let the battle begin. A hundred bucks to anyone that

can beat me!' Brennan cried. He banged at the table with his fist until the first of the Sherpas stripped off his shirt and came in for the test.

The commotion had brought Sasha into the tent and she stood smiling indulgently in the doorway sipping a hot chocolate as the fights began.

Tenzing, the Everest veteran, gave the American a run for his money, knuckles white as they gripped each other's hands. The Sherpa was blowing like a harpooned whale, the veins on his arms about to pop. But Brennan got him in the end. Lopsang was too sozzled to offer much resistance – he fell in seconds. Next came Norgay, the guy who looked after the equipment stores; he had a lot of natural strength and looked powerful in the early moments, but Brennan gradually forced his arm back and killed him off with a final explosion of raw power.

Then he turned his attention to Kami.

'How about you, Kami? Want to have a go?'

'No thank you.'

Brennan gave him a keen look.

'You don't say no to the boss,' Jamling rebuked him with a smile. A second later Jamling and Tenzing pounced on Kami and wrestled him to the floor. Chairs flew as they crashed into the corner of the tent and a flask of hot chocolate fell with a fatal crunch onto the ground.

'Bundle!' Brennan shrieked as he jumped on top of the writhing Sherpas and the whole pile collapsed in hysterical laughter as Kami's fleece and T-shirt were pulled off him.

Finally, the young Sherpa managed to extricate himself from the scrum. He stood there, bare-chested, in front of the men, breathing heavily from the mock fight. The sight of him silenced the laughter for, although he had never even seen the inside of a gym, the sixteen-year-old Sherpa had a torso which was every bit as 'ripped' as Brennan's.

'My gods!' Tenzing stepped forward and gave Kami's biceps a squeeze. 'You can beat him!'

Sasha took a photograph.

The contest began. Brennan tried a swift attack, trying to slam Kami's arm down with a quick assault. The fast move took the young Sherpa by surprise and the back of his hand hovered perilously close to the table surface for a second or two before he managed to recover.

He steeled himself and launched an audacious counter attack, giving the American a first taste of what he had to offer. The Sherpas cheered as Brennan's arm bent backwards, his knuckles white as he gripped Kami's hand for dear life.

'Way to go!' Brennan laughed at the cheek of the move but he was gradually able to force his arm back upright.

Brennan was growing red in the face. The strain of resisting Kami's assault was getting to him and his bicep had developed a telltale tremor as lactic acid began to build.

'You can do better than this,' Brennan admonished him. 'Give me the best you got.'

Kami realised the competition had reached a curious state of deadlock; he felt he could resist Brennan's strength indefinitely, perhaps even wear him down and beat him in the end. But the young Nepali's head was beginning to swim; the cries of the other Sherpas and the shouts of 'Go! Go! Go! Go!' from the Westerners were overwhelming him. He throttled back on the power for a beat or two then let Brennan slam his arm over for the victory.

'Got you!' Brennan roared. The Sherpas went wild. Sasha photographed Brennan as he did a victory jig around the tent.

Later Kami went out of the tent to the washstand. He cupped his hands and bathed his face in the cool water, then found that Brennan had followed him out. He was shoulder to shoulder, doing the same.

'Did you let me win?' Brennan asked him in a low voice. 'Cos you know that would really piss me off.'

'Perhaps it was the gods who decided.'

Brennan stared at Kami for a moment then nodded

slightly, recognising the grace of the reply. Then he wiped his hands dry on the towel and walked back to the tent.

Kami knew that something had changed but he wasn't sure what.

○

Two days of hard grafting followed. Days in which the expedition nudged closer to the five thousand metre level where the thin air would start to become a real challenge. Michael – the taciturn security guard who was supposed to be one of Brennan's bodyguards – succumbed to a case of altitude sickness. He battled on for twenty-four hours with constant nausea and a pounding headache, but it was hopeless. His body just couldn't adjust to the altitude and he was totally unable to sleep or function properly.

'Michael's going back to the States,' Brennan told the team at Pheriche. 'Kurt will handle the security from now on.'

'One down,' Jamling said quietly as they watched him move away sadly down the trail. 'Five to go!'

Other climbing teams were around them now, also with long lines of heavily laden pack animals. Sometimes they had to queue to cross the river, waiting patiently as up to a hundred yaks picked their way reluctantly across narrow bridges.

'I never thought there'd be traffic jams up here,' Kami heard Brennan say to Tenzing.

'Wait till you get into the icefall,' Tenzing replied. 'Then it gets really bad.'

That night the team camped close to the snout of the Khumbu glacier, at a scrappy lodging place called Gorak Shep. This was the last human habitation before Base Camp and it had a real frontier feel to it.

Now it was Sasha's turn to get altitude sickness – not as seriously as Michael, but badly enough to leave her exhausted.

'I'm going to stay here and rest for twenty-four hours,' she told the team. 'I'll catch you up at Base Camp.'

The next day was a day of note – the first trip up to Base Camp and a fifteen-kilometre hike up the Khumbu glacier. It was the first time that Kami had walked on such a massive glacier and he enjoyed the sensation of being on the ice, sensing the huge power of the slowly-moving monster as it ground down the valley.

The surrounding scenery was the most spectacular he had ever seen. They were now in the heartland of the Himalaya and the walls that flanked the glacier were soaring ramparts of almost vertical rock and ice. Everest was hidden from view, locked away behind the savage wall of Nuptse.

He took his camera out to take a shot, then muttered a curse as he remembered Pemba still had his memory card.

Instead, he resolved to try and imprint it all in his mind. Apart from anything else, he wanted to be able to relive the whole journey for Shreeya when he returned home. He knew she would want him to tell her absolutely everything about the expedition, both good and bad.

They had a lunch break halfway up the glacier – the Westerners dining on cheese omelettes and Spam fritters, the Sherpas wolfing down rice and lentils.

Midway through the meal Alex Brennan got a call on his satphone. His amiable mood quickly vanished as he talked, and afterwards, with a face like thunder, he summoned Kurt to his side.

'Looks like the boss got some bad news,' Tenzing commented nervously.

Kurt came over a short time later.

'Alex and I are going ahead,' he told them in clipped tones. 'There's going to be a meeting at Base Camp. Everyone has to be there.'

The unfriendly tone of the order took the Sherpas by surprise.

'What's gone wrong?' Norgay wondered aloud.

The odd encounter unsettled the group and Kami couldn't help notice that Nima had gone very quiet.

'You look like you've seen a ghost,' Kami observed.

'Must be the altitude,' Nima muttered.

There was a lot of traffic during the last two hours. Long lines of yaks and porters were moving in both directions and it felt to Kami like the trek was going on forever. But finally they came around the last graceful curve of the glacier and Base Camp was before them.

'What a place,' he remarked, struck by the forbidding vision in front of him. The stark reality of the location was very far from the romantic spot he had imagined.

Really there was nothing to distinguish it from the rest of the glacier. It just happened to be the last bit of flattish ground before the serious climbing began.

'No time to rest,' Tenzing chided them. 'We have to get the big tents up fast.'

The Sherpas wearily got to work, hauling the vast canvas tents out of their stuff sacks and assembling the metal frames. Alex and Kurt had vanished into a communications tent belonging to another team.

At 5 p.m. the team was ordered to assemble in the mess tent. The atmosphere was electric. Alex Brennan strode in ten minutes later clutching a handful of papers.

'We've got a problem,' Brennan told them sharply, 'and this is why.'

He handed out the sheets which Kami could see immediately were copies of newspapers and websites.

'We've printed these out just now,' Brennan told them, 'and I think you'll see straight away why I'm spitting mad.'

Kami stared at the printout in his hand. It was a gossip magazine article featuring a series of colour photos of Alex Brennan and Sasha. Dressed in just their bathing costumes, the snaps had caught Sasha and the boss swimming together, sunbathing side by side and even holding hands as they jumped off the boulder into the river. Straight away he realised the shots were taken on the afternoon at Pangboche and he flashed a look at Nima and Pemba who were standing nearby, both ashen-faced.

'This is exactly the type of publicity that I don't need,' Brennan continued, his voice loaded with fury, 'and I regard this as the most blatant type of betrayal.'

'Someone from the team took these and emailed them back to a journalist in the US,' Kurt snapped, 'and they've deliberately set out to take shots of Alex and Sasha together.'

Kurt was right, Kami realised. To look at the pictures you would think the boss and Sasha had been alone. Innocent fooling around had been twisted to look like something else.

The title of the piece in his hand was 'High Passion'.

'Alex's fiancée has had photographers camped out outside

her flat since these pictures went public,' Kurt went on, 'and now the shots are getting syndicated all over the world.'

Kami risked a glance at Nima. His friend looked like he was about to faint with terror. Pemba refused to meet his eye.

'So the question is very simple,' Brennan continued. 'Who took these photographs? We know it was someone from our team. There was nobody else down there that afternoon.'

Silence followed. A deep and unsettled silence in which Kami felt his stomach churning with fear.

'Own up,' Kurt ordered.

'I don't think it could be one of the Sherpas ... ' Tenzing said. But his voice lacked conviction.

'It most certainly was one of your team,' Brennan countered angrily, 'and we're going to find out who if it takes us all night.'

The silence resumed. Kami stared again at Pemba but all he got back was a dirty look. The Sherpas shuffled their feet. Wind ruffled the canvas of the tent.

'There's another simple way we can approach this,' Kurt said. 'Who's got a camera?'

Kami felt like a noose was slowly tightening around his neck; he knew all too well that the shots had been taken on his camera. Norgay and Lopsang raised their hands. Kami also, his arm shaking.

'Tenzing, will you go and fetch their packs please,' Kurt ordered.

The rucksacks were fetched and the cameras pulled out and placed on the mess tent table. The assembled Sherpas moved in tighter to the table, craning their necks to see.

'Anyone mind if we check the memory cards?' Kurt asked.

Lopsang and Norgay grunted their assent but Kami blurted out, 'There's no memory card in mine. It went missing ... '

Kurt flipped open the little plastic catch on Kami's camera.

'There is one,' he said. 'You must be mistaken.'

Kami felt his face flush red with shock and confusion. Pemba or Nima must have replaced the card in secret, he quickly surmised. He felt the eyes of everyone present boring into him.

Kurt switched the camera on and started screening the shots.

'Bingo,' he said.

He twisted the camera so that Kami could see the pictures – the same ones that had appeared in the magazine. The others erupted in a buzz of excited chatter.

Kami felt like a great pit had just opened up beneath his feet. Bile rose in his throat.

'This is your last chance, Kami,' Brennan told him emphatically. 'If someone borrowed your camera that afternoon then you have to tell us the name.'

Kami felt tears pricking at the back of his eyes. It was all happening so quickly. And there was so much at stake. He felt the raw conflict of the moment. If it had just been Pemba he might have blurted out his name. But it wasn't; it was Nima as well, someone who – despite everything – he still regarded as a friend.

And if there was one thing that Kami could not do it was betray a friend.

Kami shook his head. Jamling and Tenzing let out an audible gasp of disappointment.

'That's it,' Brennan said. 'I had high hopes for you on this expedition, Kami, but you've really let me down. I want you to pack up your things and leave right away. You're off the team.'

O

Kami staggered out onto the glacier. He felt dizzy and disorientated. The sense of injustice burned like some exotic torture.

The gods had deserted him. Just when he needed them most. He had never felt more alone.

Shock quickly overwhelmed him. The dream that had sustained him through the long winter had been cut away and discarded like an amputated limb. What would he do now? How would he ever pluck up the courage to walk back into his village? To face those he loved and tell them of his disgrace?

How could he possibly face Shreeya, knowing that this blow would end all their dreams of a life together?

'You can go in the morning if you like,' Lakhpa told him sympathetically. 'It's too late to be wandering down the glacier now.'

'No,' Kami countered. 'I'll go now.'

'But your money … ' Tenzing called. 'I have to pay you what you're owed up to today.'

'Give it to the monks at Tengboche,' Kami told him earnestly. 'It's no good to me now.'

He picked up his things. He swung the pack onto his back and set off down the glacier, wanting nothing but to put the team and Base Camp far behind him. His mind was seething with a poisonous concoction of anger and self-pity. How could this have happened to him? Why didn't Nima step forward to say what had really happened?

As for Pemba, well Kami felt nothing but contempt.

The day was darkening, the cold clamping down as the sun was banished. After a while he heard a voice calling out behind him. In the late afternoon gloom he could just make out it was Nima, some distance behind, following him down the glacier.

'Kami!' Nima yelled. 'Come back! I'm sorry!'

But Kami blocked his ears to the cries, putting on more pace. He was too distressed to talk, the pain was too raw. And in any case – he thought – what could Nima say that could possibly help?

He came to a split in the track and, on an impulse, took the right-hand trail which he knew would take him across to the other side of the glacier. Beyond that, the trail led to Kala Pattar – a trekking peak which was famous for its grandstand view of Everest's summit.

He reached the slope – and began to climb at frantic speed. Next time he looked back Nima was just a tiny dot far back on the glacier and as darkness fell he saw his pursuer turn back for Base Camp.

The night was clear and exceptionally cold. The moon rose over the nearby peak of Pumori, casting a silvery wash of light over the Khumbu valley and giving him just enough vision to climb by. Kami kept on, driven by a wave of conflicting emotions, not stopping until midnight when he reached the little cairn that marked the high point.

There, at almost six thousand metres, he wrapped his sleeping bag around him and turned his eyes to the stunning night vista. The top section of Everest was standing proud on the inky-black horizon, the snows of the high gullies glittering with dim blue light.

He gazed on that sacred summit and his mind began to churn.

Why had things gone so wrong?

Were the gods teaching him a lesson?

More than anything, Kami felt the keen edge of total humiliation. He had lost all face. Been exposed, utterly unfairly, as the guilty perpetrator of a sordid and shameful incident. In the process he had let so many people down, Jamling above all.

Kami was gutted to think about it. And he had the terrible feeling he would be thinking about it every day of the rest of his life.

He would be crawling home like a cockroach. Shamed and belittled as a liar and a cheat. There would be no money to pay off Laxmi's father. No possibility of making Shreeya his bride.

The very thought of it was enough to make him weep.

His frenzied thoughts slowed as the dead of night enveloped him. The hours stretched long and hard as forty degrees of frost wrapped Kami in an icy embrace. Swaddled in his sleeping bag he survived the night, although he did not sleep.

Instead he stared all night at the summit of Everest, fearing that this would be the nearest that he would ever get.

The very idea that he would be able to leave Shreeya's shrine bell on the top of the world now seemed little more than a cruel joke.

Nevertheless he held the bell close inside the sleeping bag, getting some consolation from the thought of Shreeya's love.

At 6 a.m Kami knew he had to get moving. His locked-up joints creaked and cracked as they flexed.

The frigid, motionless hours had frozen him to the marrow. He was walking on autopilot as he descended to the glacier, his mind drifting away in a haze of fatigue as his legs plodded on.

He regained the main track which would take him away from Everest and started to trek listlessly along it. Hunger was biting hard but he didn't care. Kami was in such a daze that he hardly noticed the two trekkers coming up the glacier.

'Kami? You OK?'

The sound of his name gave him a shock. Kami suddenly realised it was Sasha standing in front of him, a porter by her side.

'You look half dead,' Sasha told him with concern. 'Would you like some tea?'

Kami slumped down for a rest and watched as Sasha brought out her trekking flask. The drink was sweet and energising, warming his body core and bringing him back to life.

'You going down to pick up some gear?' she asked.

'No. They took me off the team,' he told her miserably.

'What? How come?'

Kami began to relate the tale, starting with the photos.

'I know about them,' Sasha interrupted him. 'My editor called me yesterday to warn me about it. That's why I decided to cut my rest short and come straight up to Base Camp to talk to Alex.'

'I got the blame for it,' Kami told her. 'It *was* my camera and ... '

'But you didn't take those photos!' Sasha exclaimed. 'Pemba did!'

Kami felt a tiny surge of hope kindle inside him.

'I remember it absolutely,' Sasha continued. 'I thought it

was a bit weird the way that Pemba was creeping around, hiding behind trees and rocks, taking shots of me and Alex.'

'But it was my camera,' Kami said miserably, 'so I'm still going to be blamed.'

Sasha fixed him with her most direct gaze.

'Kami, look at me and just tell me the truth. Did you know the camera was going to be used for that purpose?'

'No.'

'So Pemba took it without your permission?'

'Yes.' Kami felt a great surge of relief as he said that single emphatic word.

'Stand up,' she told him. 'We're going right back up to Base Camp and I'm going to put Alex straight on this.'

'I think it is too late to change things,' he said doubtfully.

'I don't think so, Kami,' Sasha told him firmly. 'You've taken the rap for something that's not your fault and now we're going to put things right.'

Sasha was good to her word. By the close of that day she had indeed put things right and – after an intense re-examining of the evidence – Kami was back on the team.

'I think we got it wrong,' Alex conceded to Kami with a smile. 'I'm happy to have you back onboard.'

Kami emerged from the tent feeling like he had been granted a second life. He performed a small puja and rang

Shreeya's bell to signify his thanks to the gods.

Pemba and Nima were grilled at length by Kurt, Alex and Sasha. Pemba was sacked from the expedition. He left in bad grace, scattering foul curses at Westerners and Sherpas alike as he packed his stuff and ran off towards Gorak Shep.

Nima was given a second chance. He obviously wasn't entirely innocent, everyone realised, but he hadn't been the one to steal the camera, take the shots, or email them to the USA so there was little evidence to nail him with.

'I'll be watching you,' Alex Brennan told Nima sternly. 'One more problem and you are going back to Namche, you understand?'

'Yes, sir.'

After the inquisition, and his swift re-instatement, Kami walked into the mess tent feeling bruised and uncertain of how the others would treat him. But the welcome was warm, particularly from Tenzing and Jamling.

'Put it behind you,' Jamling advised him. 'There's plenty of work to do now.'

O

A number of shake-down days followed; acclimatisation time in which the Western team members recovered from the trek. They were given buckets of warm water to shower with, and encouraged to drink prodigious amounts of tea and hot chocolate.

Kami had a different brief; his days were spent with Nima, shuttling backwards and forwards to the 'clean' area of the glacier and harvesting fresh ice for the expedition water supply. They were given a sledgehammer and a sharpened steel bar to tackle the task.

It was dangerous and exhausting work; one of them had to hold the steel bar in place as it was smashed deep into the ice with the sledgehammer. A badly aimed shot would have meant a shattered wrist at the very least.

They wrapped the bigger chunks of ice in a tarpaulin and lugged them laboriously back to Lopsang's boiling cauldron.

Time and time again.

One week after arriving at Base Camp, a puja ceremony was held to placate the gods and afterwards Tenzing got the whole Sherpa team together;

'The icefall is open,' he told them with pride. 'I want the following six men to carry up to Camp One tomorrow.'

Kami's name was on the list. He tried to play it cool, not showing much reaction to the order, at least not in front of the rest of the Sherpas for whom such a request was routine. But he was blushing with quiet pride as he savoured the moment.

This was what he had been hoping for. It meant he was no longer one of the yak boys. He was one of the climbing Sherpa team. On probation, almost certainly, but Kami was determined not to let Jamling down.

Kami wrote a letter to Shreeya that night. He had intended to make it an exhaustive account of everything that had happened to date, but in the end it turned out to be short and sweet – the nearest thing to a love letter he had ever written.

It was remarkable how all the stress dissolved away as he put his feelings and passion into words.

Just the thought that she would hold the fragile scrap of paper in her hand before the week was out filled Kami with a sense of longing which surprised him with its intensity.

He sealed the missive and gave it to one of the mail runners.

The Everest climb was about to begin.

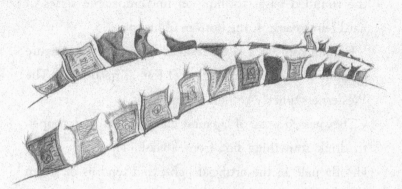

CHAPTER 7

4.45 a.m the next day. It was blowing hard as Kami joined Jamling outside the tent along with Alex Brennan, Sasha and Kurt. The night air was filled with cloud and it was cold enough to numb his lips. Snow granules were beginning to pitter against the Gore-Tex of his hood and he half expected the veteran Sherpa to call off the load carry in favour of another day.

'All set?' Jamling asked.

Evidently a snow squall wasn't going to put him off.

Kami nodded and swung his load onto his back. There were at least six oxygen cylinders inside the pack and he reckoned he was carrying thirty kilos or more. The metal tubes clunked as he began the trek up the glacier, the rounded bases forming an uncomfortable series of hard bumps against the bottom of his spine.

Jamling kept up a fast but steady pace, his squat figure pinpointed in the quartz beam of Kami's head torch. The Westerners quickly got left behind.

They passed a pair of Japanese climbers who had stopped to drink something hot from a flask. Their faces were ghostly pale in the artificial light; thin tendrils of steam rising from their shared cup. Kami got a tantalising whiff of sweet chocolate as they passed.

At the edge of the icefall Jamling stopped and shrugged off his rucksack.

'We have to kit up now,' he said.

Kami pulled out his crampons, grateful that he had practised for this moment; he snapped the sharp metal teeth straight onto the correct place on his boot without hesitation. With these vital bits of kit he would be stable on the ice, his feet unlikely to slip.

Jamling grunted his approval as he saw the expert way he did it.

Kami wrapped the ice-axe sling around his wrist and the two climbers moved off the easy ground of the glacier and entered the icefall. For Kami it was a thrilling moment – the first few steps when he could really consider that he was *on* Everest. Not just looking at it from afar, not dreaming of it, but really a part of it.

His climb had begun and he felt his body begin to warm up as the gradient quickly sharpened.

Kami was aware that the world they were now entering was loaded with the potential for sudden death. The icefall was a tortured place, gravity and the turbulent geology of the underlying rock having twisted the glacier far out of shape.

It is a bit like the penny falls in an amusement arcade; here something eases, there something pushes. A bit more pressure. A touch more stress. And the coin drops; except here in the icefall it is not a penny at all – it's a block of ice the size of a five-storey building.

The bodies of icefall victims are seldom found. They normally lie beneath many hundreds or even thousands of tons of frozen debris, a quantity that not even the most determined army of men could shovel aside.

Little wonder that this stage of the Everest climb inspired such fear.

Over the previous days a specialised Sherpa team had been busy marking the route; a series of bamboo sticks – each with a small red pennant attached – had been placed to mark the safest path through the maze of séracs, those terrifying and unstable blocks of glacial ice that towered on every side.

The terrain was so treacherous that even a seemingly solid surface could collapse without warning. But there was plenty of fixed rope and Kami was diligent in clipping his short 'cow's tail' sling onto the fixed lines, his karabiner sliding along the 9mm cords with a faint hum of metal on nylon.

As they penetrated deeper into the icefall the snow storm petered out and the sky slowly lightened as a reluctant dawn broke through. It was a gloomy, sullen start to the day, a glowering headwall of grey cloud hanging over the Khumbu valley and obscuring the high peaks.

Soon they came to the first of the big crevasses – the massive cracks that are common on fast-moving glaciers. There was no route around the huge slot and the icefall Sherpas had bridged it with three sections of ladder.

Climbers from other teams were queuing to cross, forcing Kami and Jamling to wait. As they did so, Alex Brennan and the other Westerners caught them up.

'Mind if we go first?' Alex asked them brusquely. 'I want to burn it up to Camp One as fast as I can.'

'Fine by us,' Jamling told him.

Brennan went out onto the ladders, crossing the crevasse with scarcely a pause as he forged quickly ahead. Kurt followed across – just as fast.

'He is in big hurry!' Jamling observed.

'He wants to get on the satphone,' Sasha told them grimly. 'Damage limitation.'

'Damage?' Kami asked. 'More bad things about the ... photos?'

He still had this terrible feeling that the Pemba photo incident would come back again to haunt him.

'Nothing to do with you, Kami,' Sasha assured him. 'A fax arrived back at Base. His popularity rating slipped in the polls.'

'I'm sorry. I don't understand.'

'As soon as Alex gets back to the States he'll be competing against a much more experienced politician to win his party's nomination. It's a sort of battle called the Primaries and the winner gets the chance to try to be president.'

'Ah. Very important thing.'

'Exactly. And up until now Alex has always been the most popular candidate. But yesterday a poll came out and his rival is storming ahead.'

'That's why he's angry.' Kami couldn't help feeling a sense of relief.

'Yep. His enemy is saying Alex doesn't care about the American people. That he's only interested in having an adventure on Everest thousands of miles away and not doing anything about the problems at home.'

'I see.' Kami was surprised that anyone would want to attack Alex Brennan.

Jamling checked his watch.

'Time to move,' he said. 'Kami, you go first.'

Kami did as he was ordered, then took a tentative step out onto the ladder, his steel crampon spikes skittering alarmingly against the first of the aluminium rungs. It was a perilous balancing act, he realised, particularly with such a heavy load on his back.

Alex and Kurt had had no such load and they had made it look easy.

Three more steps; now he could feel the whole contraption bouncing wildly up and down. Logic told him that he was safe. Even if he fell he would merely dangle from the safety line until he could regain the ladder.

Assuming that the safety line held.

'Go for it, Kami!' Sasha yelled.

'Don't hang around!' Jamling called out with a laugh.

Looking down was a beginner's mistake. Kami wasn't especially liable to vertigo but the inky-blue depths of the slot made his head spin. Somewhere down there, he imagined, it must narrow to a bone crushing point.

He clasped his right hand to the breast pocket of his wind suit, feeling the reassuring outline of the shrine bell.

'Get a move on,' Jamling yelled.

He hurried up the rising incline of the second and third ladders and made it to the far lip. Five minutes later Sasha and Jamling were by his side and, after a brief rest to eat some chocolate, the three of them continued following the marker wands through the icefall.

In the hours that followed they tackled two more big crevasse crossings and one almost vertical ice face which had been fixed with no fewer than five ladders.

On one of the crossings a sudden splintering noise startled Kami out of his trance. A chunk of ice the size of a minibus had popped off the wall of the crevasse and shattered into the depths.

Kami uttered a murmured prayer to the gods as they climbed out of the final chaos of ice onto the smoother terrain of the Western Cwm – the name given to the vast valley which leads to the higher camps of Everest.

They could see Camp One waiting just a few hundred metres off.

'I'm going to file my report,' Sasha told them. She gave them both a cheery wave and disappeared into a tent to write her daily article.

Kami took his load to the equipment store, proud to have made it through the icefall. But if he was looking for praise he was in the wrong place. In any case the clock was ticking, as usual, and Jamling was quickly urging him to drink up his tea and get a move on.

'We don't stay here?' Kami asked in surprise.

'No. We're back to Base now.'

On went the empty packs. Farewells shouted to the cooks and Sherpas who would remain at the camp. Then they turned back down the fixed ropes, swallowed up once again by the icefall and praying for safe passage back down to Base Camp.

The lights of Base Camp were visible by 7 p.m. Less than thirty minutes later Kami was perched on a wobbly wooden stool at the rough mess table. A piping-hot meal of rice and tinned beans was served. Kami quickly drank about four cups of salted tea as he enjoyed the Sherpa chat about the day.

Kami felt his head getting heavier. He folded his arms on the table and thought he would just take a brief nap.

He woke up in the same position, freezing cold and stiff, at 6 a.m when Lopsang started up the morning stoves.

O

Kami got a day's 'rest' after that first round trip through the icefall. He spent it running from one chore to another as

Tenzing kept him on the go. In the morning he sharpened crampon spikes with a whetstone and sewed up some damaged wind suits. In the afternoon he peeled forty kilos of potatoes and helped rescue a yak that had fallen into a glacial stream half an hour down the glacier.

He did the work with good grace but his mind was distracted with the delicious prospect of going back on the mountain. Back up high. The taste had been intoxicating. He was waiting for someone to tell him if he was needed for more porter duties.

Alex Brennan and the other Westerners had come back down after their acclimatisation stay in Camp One and the next push would go up higher.

'Will you take me back up?' Kami asked Jamling eagerly that evening, when nothing had been said all day.

Jamling laughed. 'Don't worry. You'll be going up and down like an idiot before long.'

He was right. Brennan called the whole team into the yurt at eight the next morning.

'We're going to film in the icefall today,' he said. 'Going to get a killer sequence for the news outlets. I'll need at least eight porters for all the equipment. We're taking the mini crane, the whole shebang.'

Much to his delight, Kami was picked as one of the

carrying team. He was paired up with Nima and instructed to follow the film crew, lugging the extendable crane arm up into the icefall. The metal structure weighed a hefty thirty kilos and was a cumbersome body length long.

Nima was in a grouchy mood.

'We'll be hanging around all day up there,' he complained to Kami, 'waiting for lumps of ice to fall on our heads while they mess about with the cameras.'

'Maybe they'll get it done fast,' Kami suggested, at which Nima gave a sarcastic snort.

The morning dragged by, bitterly cold and windy, as shot after shot got ticked off the sequence list. George and his sound recordist set up a whole bunch of positions in and around the spectacular ice formations, shooting Alex as he made his way through the séracs.

'They're making it look like he's on his own,' Kami remarked.

'Pah!' Nima was contemptuous. 'That's typical. It's us guys that do all the donkey work but you watch that film in the end and there'll hardly be a Sherpa in it.'

A huge ladder crossing came next, Kami and Nima performing a sort of high-wire double act as they shouldered the crane arm across. They got a round of applause from the waiting team and Brennan told them, 'You guys are going to get a bonus for this. This is service beyond the call of duty.'

Kami was pleased to hear it. Every dollar he could earn was a dollar closer to paying off his marriage contract.

Lunchtime passed with no food; the afternoon was drifting on and there were still shots to do. The temperature had dropped by about five degrees and everyone was getting increasingly chilled from standing around. Brennan began to talk with George about the final shots which would be filmed from the bottom of a crevasse.

'I want you to get down that slot,' the boss requested, 'get me crossing from below.'

'Great idea!' George was all for it.

'You'll need protection,' Tenzing said. 'We'll get a couple of the lads to rig you up a ladder at the bottom so you can move around safely.'

Nima and Kami were picked for the task and two ropes were secured at the lip.

Nima walked to the edge of the gaping crevasse with supreme confidence. He abseiled into the gaping void with the practised air of someone who had done it a hundred times before.

Kami took the plunge next, less confident, but still managing to do a good job of it as the rest of the team looked on.

The temperature shift was shocking. The interior of the crevasse was way colder than up top. Kami felt himself shiver and wished he had thought to put on an extra layer.

Ten metres down. Fifteen. Kami felt he was descending into a bizarre blue universe as the glacial ice of the walls gradually tapered to a sinister, body crushing 'V'.

'Lock off the line,' Nima told him. Kami slipped the rope over the descender and stabilised himself. He looked up, seeing the row of tiny faces peering down at them. He tried to guess how deep they were; twenty metres, perhaps more?

Deep in the belly of the monster. His breath was freezing on his lips.

'OK. Send it down,' Nima shouted.

The single length of aluminium ladder was lowered down and Nima explained the plan.

'We'll wedge the ladder across the gap,' he said. 'The camera guy can use it as a platform.'

Kami quickly saw the logic of the plan. The length of ladder was just right to form an impromptu bridge across the narrow part of the slot.

They cut some grooves in the ice, smashing with their axes at the rock hard surface, sharp blue chips tumbling down into the depths. Next, they swung the ladder into position, the legs slotting into the holes neatly.

'You see?' Nima said, tapping the ladder proudly. 'He can sit on it, stand on it. Do what he wants.'

The bulky silhouette of George soon appeared over the lip, swinging out over the drop. He didn't look too comfortable, his feet kicking clumsily at the wall as he went down into the abyss.

'Man, it's like the lost world in here!' he shouted up. 'You guys don't know what you're missing.'

'You're welcome to it,' Brennan called down.

The ladder creaked as George's weight came onto it, but the ice slots looked solid and safe. He kept his life line on for good measure though as he set up for the shots.

Kami had noticed before that the filming always seemed to take an age, but this time was worse than ever. The two of them were shivering non-stop now the cold had really got to them.

George was better equipped in a down suit and he hardly seemed to be feeling it.

Boom! A huge retort rendered the frigid air of the crevasse. It really sounded like a cannon going off and Kami felt himself jump with the shock of it. He looked at Nima for reassurance but his friend also looked freaked by the noise.

Small stalactites of frozen ice fell off the crevasse walls as the ground shook. Something huge had fallen ... somewhere.

At long last George pronounced himself ready.

'Get Alex to go across on his own,' he yelled up. 'I'm running.'

'OK!'

Brennan started to make his way across the ladder. Kami could see that the shot would be special.

'Epic!' George yelled up. 'Now get him to go back again and do it again a bit slower.'

Then came the tight shot. Then he changed the lens for a super wide angle. Fifteen minutes after that he was done. The camera was hauled up and a pair of jumars – special clamps that enable climbers to move vertically up a rope – were sent down so they could escape the crevasse.

'Let him come up first,' Tenzing yelled down to the two Sherpa lads, 'There's some sunset shots they want to do back at Base Camp and we're running late.'

'OK,' Nima agreed. Kami's lips were chattering so hard he couldn't have replied.

George began the climb and Kami realised straight away that he wasn't going to be fast. He lunged up in a clumsy style, pushing the jumar clamp up in small, inefficient bursts of energy.

'He's taking forever,' Nima whispered. Kami felt the tip of his nose going completely numb.

Half an hour went by. Another half an hour for the cold to penetrate a little deeper. Half an hour for fingertips and toes to succumb.

Finally, George got close to the top; two pairs of hands reached over the lip of the crevasse and he was dragged out on his belly.

'At last!' Nima exclaimed. 'Now hurry please! Send down the gear, we're freezing down here!'

A further unexplained delay occurred. Kami guessed they were filming something up top. The crevasse gave out a few more ghostly groans as the ice flexed – it really was getting Kami quite spooked. Then, finally, the gear was sent down to the two boys.

'You want to go first?' Kami asked his friend.

'Of course I *want* to,' Nima snapped, 'but you go.'

He handed the kit over. Kami stamped his feet on the ladder, trying to shock his toes back into life. Then he strapped on the chest harness and began to ascend the rope. He felt his hands begin to thaw out, the dull pain of the hot aches causing him to swear beneath his breath.

'Come on! We have to get out here!' Nima urged him.

As Kami ascended he noticed something curious; he could no longer hear the voices of the others up top. He figured they must be filming.

Nima was now a tiny figure beneath him, little more than a dark shadow really at the bottom of the slot.

'You OK?' Kami called down.

'No,' Nima uttered.

Kami summoned some more energy from somewhere and put on a burst of movement. He hauled himself up the small overhang, rolled onto the ice and rested for a few seconds as he looked around in surprise.

There was no one there at all. The whole team had hurried back down to Base Camp.

It wasn't what he expected. He had thought Tenzing would leave at least a couple of his men to help them. But no. There was no welcoming voice to greet him. No friendly hand to help him up.

The sun had long since crashed below the ridge. He reckoned there was just an hour to dusk. He couldn't even hear the voices of the descending team. The icefall felt desolate and threatening.

'They've all gone,' he yelled down the crevasse.

'Whatever. Just send down the gear.' Nima's voice was curiously thin, and Kami thought he could detect a tinge of desperation in it.

'OK.'

He unclipped the jumar clamps and the chest harness, but his fingers were still partly frozen and he messed up.

'Look out!'

The two jumars slipped out of his grasp, bounced once, then slipped down the angled ice into the crevasse.

'Catch them!' he yelled.

But it was already too late. It had all happened too fast. The gear had dropped in a flash, out of Nima's reach, through the narrowest part of the fissure and into the dark interior of the glacier.

'Was that what I think it was?' Nima called up. There was a hollow ring of despair in his tone.

'Yes, I ... '

Nima bawled him out with a vicious string of swear words. He raged and cursed Kami in a way that he had never been cursed before. Kami listened, aghast. He had never felt so clumsy and hamfisted.

'I'm so sorry ... ' he stammered.

'Try and pull me up,' Nima cried. He tried to climb hand over hand up the rope, his crampons kicking hopelessly into the steely ice wall. Kami clutched the rope and bent his entire force to the task, but was unable to pull his friend up even a single metre.

Nima called for him to stop.

'You'll have to catch them up,' he yelled. 'Get some more jumars. Quickly, Kami. Quickly!'

Kami yelled some words of encouragement to Nima and started to race down the icefall.

He knew he was taking risks but what choice did he have? Every extra minute that Nima was imprisoned in that ice was a minute in hell.

Would Nima get frostbite down there? Hypothermia? Could he even freeze to death? Kami pushed himself to move faster and faster, sliding down the vertical ladders, crashing into the soft snow at the base, rushing across the crevasse bridges without even tying on.

He was pushing his body too hard. A sort of oxygen deficit began to set in; he felt giddy, sick with a toxic concoction of hypoxia and fear. He experienced an urgent need to stop and defecate but that was out of the question.

The awful moment went round and round in his head. How had he ever been so stupid? So ham-fisted. Dropping those jumars over the edge revealed what he really was; a hopeless beginner, the worst type of amateur.

He stopped for a beat, let out a cry: 'Tenzing! Stop!'

A fractured echo bounced back mockingly from the west flank. No response. He began to move again. Following the wands. Jumping the smaller slots. Taking chances that the snow bridges would hold. Feeling the treacherous bounce of the ladders as the depths yawned beneath.

Every time he rounded a sérac he expected to see the retreating figures of the expedition. But they had half an hour's head start on him and were moving fast. The maze was empty and time was racing with unreasonable speed.

Then he saw them. Just a few hundred metres from the rocky edge of the glacier.

'Hey!' Kami screamed. He put so much force into the yell he thought his tonsils might get blasted out of his throat.

Tenzing turned. He waited as Kami caught up. The team gathered round as he gasped out the story.

Then Kami felt his vision narrow in the most disturbing way. Flashing shapes were gathering in at the edges of his world. The glacier was actually turning black. Someone offered him a water bottle but he couldn't co-ordinate his arm to reach up and grab it.

Kami fainted there and then, flat out on the ice.

○

He awoke the next morning at Base Camp, lying on top of a sleeping bag, still dressed in his mountain gear. It took his mind a few moments to focus, then images came to him; blacking out in the icefall, the stumbling descent to Base Camp, Sasha and the boss supporting him. His arms around their shoulders.

Nima. He sat up abruptly. *Had they managed to extract him from the crevasse? Where was he now?*

Kami unzipped the tent and found Jamling outside.

'Is he OK?' he asked.

Jamling spat out a gobbet of tobacco juice.

'More or less,' he said laconically.

Kami slipped on his boots and headed for the mess tent.

Lopsang was frying up Spam fritters in a pan, the smell of the sizzling meat reminding Kami that he hadn't eaten since the previous morning. He bolted down three plates while Tenzing filled him in on the rescue.

'We got back up there as fast as we could,' Tenzing said, 'but he was frozen half to death. He couldn't use his hands at all so we had to strap him to the ladder and haul him up like that.'

Kami tried to imagine the scene, a wave of shame and guilt engulfing him. Then he tried to figure how long Nima had been there alone. It must have been two hours. Maybe three. He shuddered at the thought of it.

'He was talking with the fairies by that point,' Tenzing continued. 'Hypothermia had got him. We sledged him down the icefall, then warmed him up here for a couple of hours. Then I had a couple of guys walk him through the night down to Pheriche.'

'Where is he now?'

'At the clinic. One of his hands is frostbitten.'

'I want to see him,' Kami told Tenzing. 'Can you give me a couple of days off?'

Tenzing considered the request for a few seconds.

'It's going to be tricky … ' He replied. 'Nima's obviously off the expedition now so we're down a man. The boss is getting more and more stressed and we've got more than fifty loads to shift through the icefall in the next few days. I can't really let you go.'

'I'll do double carries when I get back,' Kami promised. 'Give me twenty-four hours off. Please.'

'OK. I guess … but if you take longer I'll have to find someone else to take your place.'

Kami felt a bit sick as he heard that. He knew there were plenty of strong lads just like him, waiting – jobless – down at Gorak Shep and Lobuche, ready to step into his shoes. But the need to see Nima was more than he could resist.

'I'll be back very fast,' he promised. Then he ran to his tent to prepare a small pack with some gear.

'Hey,' Tenzing called out, 'I'm sorry we left you like that. That was my mistake. I should have told a couple of guys to wait, made sure you got out OK.'

'OK,' Kami replied. 'I appreciate that.'

Tenzing's apology was a consolation of sorts. It gave Kami a way to rationalise what had happened. Yes, it had been his fault entirely that the gear had been dropped. But the whole reason it happened was that his own hands were frozen from waiting while George got his shots.

But such mind games were futile. He still blamed himself and he found the incident churned over and over in his head for the entire twenty-kilometre trek down the Khumbu glacier to Pheriche.

He did the march in six hours. When he arrived he asked around for the clinic, introduced himself to one of the nurses and waited nervously to be shown into Nima's room.

Then she came back and told him, 'I'm afraid he doesn't want to see you.'

Kami was crushed by this.

His instinct was to rush into the room anyway but he figured that might only make things worse. Instead he sat in the reception area of the clinic and wrote a note for Nima. He pleaded for forgiveness and begged for a chance to make amends.

The nurse agreed to take it but she came back three minutes later and it was ripped to pieces.

'I think you should go,' she told him. 'It's only making him stressed to know you are here.'

Kami waited for a couple more hours but, finally, he gave it up. He had to get back to the expedition and he knew he couldn't force Nima to see him if he didn't want to.

He wrote Nima a final note and told the nurse he was leaving. But, just as he was passing the side of the clinic he saw movement.

A pale face stared out at him. Dark, accusing eyes framed in the splintering wooden frame of the window.

As Kami watched, mesmerised, Nima slowly brought his hand up to the glass. The fingers were absolutely black, horribly swollen.

He looked at Kami in a venomous way for a few seconds then drew the curtain back across the window.

Kami suddenly got the most terrible premonition that he would never see his friend again.

CHAPTER 8

Two days later Kami was back into the icefall. Once again it was a dawn departure. Once again he was with Jamling, and this time the danger zone seemed like familiar ground. The problem was the load; a huge great bundle of spindly aluminium struts and poles which would form a mess tent higher in the Cwm. No matter how he tied them up together, the individual poles kept slipping out of the bunch in the most irritating and dangerous way.

On the longer crevasse crossings he had a new fear to contend with; if one of the poles tumbled into the depths he would be in deep trouble with Tenzing.

'Better you than me,' Jamling said as he watched Kami's struggle. His own load was a lot friendlier – a generator to power Alex Brennan's satphone at Camp Two – and was 'light' by Sherpa standards, at a mere twenty-two kilogrammes.

There was more traffic in the icefall this time. They had to queue to get onto some of the ladder crossings, waiting for nervous Western climbers to cross the wobbling bridges.

'This is dangerous,' Jamling observed as they joined yet another line. 'Every moment we hang around in this place is another moment to get hurt.'

Gradually they found ways to overtake the slower-moving climbers, pushing to the front of the pack and making it through the last of the crevasses by midday.

Kami felt his mood lighten as he saw the tents of Camp One. This time he would be staying there, and going higher the next day.

But as they approached the Camp, a sérac peeled away from the cliff above with an impressive WHUMPH. The debris gathered pace with terrifying speed as it cascaded down the face and to Kami's inexperienced eyes it seemed they would surely be engulfed.

'That's OK,' Jamling reassured him. 'No need to run. Just powder.'

The two of them stood their ground as the leading edge of the avalanche billowed across the glacier towards them.

There was a moment when Kami felt that Jamling must surely be mistaken, that the cloud would contain pulverising blocks of snow and ice.

But his judgement had been spot on and the true force of the avalanche had been dissipated at the foot of the face. Now it was ice crystals and nothing more. The world went white for a few minutes as the pulverised ice swirled around them. Then it gradually settled, leaving just a milky haze in the air.

Kami dozed in his tent through the afternoon and at supper time he put his boots back on and hurried through sleeting snow to join the others.

'How about some Sherpa music?' Sasha requested.

'A pleasure!' Jamling exclaimed. A silver mouth organ slipped into his hand and he began to play.

Kami listened in surprise as Jamling did his stuff. He had never thought of his mentor as an artistic man but he really played with skill, coaxing haunting Tibetan folk songs out of the little instrument.

Kami found himself thinking about Shreeya and feeling mightily homesick. If only she could see him now, he thought, how proud would she be?

Sitting at Camp One with the real Everest climbers. One of the team.

Kami had to share a tent with Lopsang that night. The cook snored like a pig, exhaling sour alcohol fumes that filled the little tent. Kami drowsed in a kind of stupor, but he couldn't really have called it sleep.

Tenzing shook the tent at dawn and it was full tilt into the new day, any fatigue forgotten with the busy rounds of breakfast, packing and departure.

Kami was carrying the heaviest load yet; a full pack of filming batteries, food rations, and a tripod head in a flight case that had to weigh ten kilos on its own.

'You're OK with all that gear, right?' Alex asked him as the Sherpas filed past the Westerners' mess tent.

'Very good, sir,' Kami replied, flashing him a radiant smile that gave no hint of the pain his body was experiencing.

Two hours of hard drill followed. They weaved a route through the sentinel crevasses that guarded the Cwm, then crossed over towards the southern side of the valley where the route was less prone to avalanche. Kami felt his muscles gradually warm to the task, the spectacular weight of the pack causing a slick patch of sweat in the centre of his back.

Halfway through that day's climb they came across the first of the many dead bodies that are littered about Everest's slopes.

It was a shock to Kami. A gaping skull. A skeletal claw of a hand. A wind suit bleached by ultra violet assault. Clinging fragments of flesh bearing the beak marks of scavenging birds.

'Do you know who he was?' Kami asked.

Jamling nodded sadly, 'he was a friend.'

Jamling placed a small pile of dried flower petals on the corpse.

'Why doesn't somebody take the body back to Base Camp?' Kami asked.

'Superstition,' Jamling replied. 'Would you want to touch it?'

Kami shivered at the thought. He understood perfectly what Jamling meant. The idea of touching a dead body was taboo to most Sherpa people and, besides, to extract the body from the ice would be a gruesome task, a question of chipping out bones, ripping out flesh.

At that moment the Western climbing team caught them up.

'Oh my goodness.' Sasha put her hand to her mouth in shock as she saw the mutilated remains. 'That is a terrible sight.'

'We need this for the film,' the boss said dispassionately. George nodded his agreement and they began to prep the film gear.

Jamling and Kami exchanged a glance.

'They should not be filming him,' Jamling muttered.

Kami nodded his agreement.

'Maybe you should tell them he was your friend?' Kami whispered.

'I don't know … ' Jamling was reluctant to interrupt the filming.

Kami watched as Alex kneeled next to the corpse and began a piece to camera.

'This is just one of the many dozens of dead bodies we are likely to encounter here on the slopes of Everest … There's no telling who this man was, or how he died, but … '

Kami felt terrible for Jamling. It was totally insensitive to film the remains of his friend in this way. Finally, he plucked up his courage.

'Erm, sir. I think Jamling would like to say something,' he blurted out.

'Cut!' The sound recordist glared at Kami.

'Don't interrupt while we're doing a shot,' Brennan snapped.

'We'll have to do it again,' George said angrily.

'Don't you think we should listen to what they have to say?' Sasha asked Brennan.

'All right,' he conceded reluctantly. 'Tell me the problem Jamling.'

But Jamling just froze. He couldn't think of the words to say. And Kami didn't want to further antagonise the boss.

'Let's go again,' George said. 'I'm getting cold here.'

They shot the rest of the sequence, packed up the gear and moved on.

Kami felt a bit nauseous as he stepped over the dessicated corpse. The filming thing had unsettled him deeply, not least because the boss had been so unmoved by the pile of bones and frozen flesh. Was this what the mountain did to you? Squeeze all the humanity out of your soul?

'What was Jamling wanting to say back there?' Sasha asked him gently.

Kami told her.

'That's terrible,' she exclaimed. 'Alex really should have had more patience with you. Talked it through.'

Later Kami heard her remonstrating with the boss although he didn't seem to have much to say in response.

Kami pulled out the shrine bell and placed it inside his glove, the metal warming against the flesh of his palm for the rest of that morning as he dutifully followed the others up the Cwm.

He found it gave him strength.

By 2 p.m the little group of Sherpas had pulled ahead of the Westerners. By 3.30 p.m. they trudged in to Camp Two.

Kami had a throbbing headache and he rushed to the mess tent and begged a litre of water. He snatched the bottle and glugged it down in one, soaking it up like a sponge as he slaked his raging thirst.

'When did you last drink?' Jamling asked him.

'This morning. Breakfast.'

'Not enough,' he snapped. 'I've told you. You won't go higher if you don't get fluid inside you.'

It was a rebuke too far. Kami felt tears prick his eyes. The day had been savagely hard and it wasn't his fault he hadn't been able to drink.

'There's news about Nima by the way,' Jamling told him.

Kami's heart leaped to hear this. 'Is he still in the hospital? Getting better?'

'No. He quit the hospital and was last seen getting drunk in a bar in Namche.'

The news was the last thing Kami wanted to hear. Nima had a reputation as a drinker and he knew his recovery would be difficult if he went off the rails.

'Tenzing should send someone down to help him,' Kami suggested.

Jamling grunted his agreement but both of them knew it wouldn't happen.

Wanting to escape the stress, Kami snuggled up in his

sleeping bag, listening to the wind plucking at the guide lines of the tent. The day had been really tough and he felt a bit gloomy and frightened. What would Shreeya tell him in such circumstances, he wondered? The words she had uttered at their final goodbye were still with him.

Don't get sad that we are apart, Kami. I will be thinking of you every moment, praying for you to come back safely.

Kami felt a comforting flood of warmth move through his body. The words replayed in his mind were so vivid, so heartfelt that it was almost as if Shreeya was there with him in the tent. Curled up by his side.

Kami didn't go to the food tent that night. Instead he slept soundly through all of the hours of darkness, waking up at first light as a blustery storm began to engulf the camp.

He came out of the tent and found Jamling and Sasha already out and dressed. Sasha was looking grim, and she plodded over through the driving snow to talk to Kami.

'Your friend Nima has been busy down in Namche,' she told him. 'Alex has been on the satellite unit and the PR situation just got a whole lot worse.'

Alex Brennan unzipped his tent and beckoned to Kami to come over.

'Have a look at this.'

He handed Kami his iPad, which was showing the front page of an online newspaper.

'LEFT TO DIE!' was the headline. Underneath it was a picture of Nima, staring angrily at the camera, his ghoulish black fingers held up close to the lens. It was certainly a striking image and Kami's heart plummeted as he realised what Nima had done.

'Go on! Read it!' Brennan exclaimed.

Kami read the following:

> Alex Brennan's Everest expedition suffered a new setback yesterday as one of his Sherpa team was evacuated from the mountain with severe frostbite. Nima Gyaltzen, 18, had been assisting on the mountain but was almost frozen to death after being abandoned in the notorious icefall.
>
> 'He was more interested in the filming,' the young Sherpa revealed. 'They forced me to go down a crevasse and then left me there for hours. He didn't care if I was dead or alive. Now they're going to have to amputate my fingers and maybe my hand.'

Kami had to stop reading at that point as he felt physically sick.

'There's plenty more where that came from,' Brennan told Kami bitterly as he flicked through other syndicated headlines and articles on the iPad – all basically carrying the same story and pictures.

'He's gone crazy,' Kami said.

'He certainly has,' Brennan agreed, 'and he's doing a good job of turning the American people completely against me.'

'Maybe it's true. We should have looked after him better,' Sasha suggested.

'You can say that now,' Brennan retorted. 'In any case we paid for the clinic and gave him a whole bunch of cash ... '

The argument ended abruptly as a huge blast of hurricane-force wind swept across the face. Other expeditions were already on the move, heading down.

'I guess that's us done for the time being,' Brennan said forlornly. 'We'll have to hang out at Camp One until the storm's over.'

The team zipped up the tents and hurriedly retreated, lost in their own worlds as they descended all the way back down the Cwm to the sanctuary of Camp One.

Kami found his mind churning over those awful pictures of Nima's deadened fingers. So much pain. So much damage.

But he found it hard to be truly sympathetic; Nima had betrayed Alex in an even more destructive way than Pemba. He wondered how much the frog man journalist had paid Nima for his story. He hoped Nima felt it was worth it.

As for the boss, well he had gone ominously silent.

'He's got a lot on his mind now,' Sasha commented to Kami, 'and the real stressful part of all this hasn't even begun.'

Kami thought about that a lot as he trekked on through the bullying wind of the blizzard.

O

The storm raged for three days, dumping a spectacular load of snow on the mountain and trapping the team at Camp One. Alex Brennan spent most of his time on the satphone, trying to put the world right on Nima's story, and firing off faxes and emails to rally his political supporters.

'The Sherpa in question has had mental issues,' Kami heard him say, over and over. 'It's really quite a sad situation but we're doing our best to help him out.'

Tension began to build. Kami felt himself irritable and jumpy, longing for the storm to end so they could escape the pressure-cooker environment of the claustrophobic camp. The other Sherpas were equally out of sorts, passing their days playing poker and sipping from bottles of cheap Chinese rum.

Kami had noticed that Sasha's relationship with Alex Brennan was getting increasingly strained. They were snapping at each other at meal times and on the second day of the storm it came to a head as she sat at the mess table writing her daily report.

'You mind if I take a look at that?' Brennan asked her casually.

Sasha blinked in surprise.

'Normally I just send it,' she said.

'I know … but would you mind if I just checked it out?'

There was an awkward pause for a few moments.

'I'm not sure I want you to … ' Sasha began.

But Brennan twisted her laptop round so he could see the article.

'That wasn't our agreement,' Sasha protested. 'In the contract it stipulates … '

'Yeah. I know what the contract says,' Brennan said brusquely. 'But I saw the piece you wrote yesterday, the bit where you said "The fault lines are beginning to show".'

'I'm just trying to paint an accurate picture,' the journalist insisted.

'Well things have changed and I can't afford any more negative publicity.'

Sasha tried to pull the laptop away from the boss but he just held it tighter as he read.

'You see. There, for example. You write "With every setback to the expedition, the necessity of reaching the summit gets stronger. The eyes of the world are on Alex Brennan now and the plain fact is that he cannot afford to fail.'''

Sasha pulled the laptop out of his hands and snapped shut the lid.

'I thought I could depend on you,' Brennan said accusingly, 'but you've changed your angle on the whole thing.'

'It's you that's changed,' Sasha counter-attacked, 'you're getting paranoid. Becoming a control freak.'

She stomped out of the mess tent.

'I'm not sure you handled that very well,' Kurt told the boss.

Brennan put his head in his hands. Kami had to avert his eyes.

When the storm finally blew itself out on the fourth day, Kami was deeply relieved. Even the prospect of hard physical grind was better than the endless hanging around.

'You come with me today,' Jamling barked at breakfast. 'Norgay can stay with the film crew.'

Kami was given a two-hundred-metre drum of climbing rope to porter up to Camp Three. Jamling had the same twenty-five-kilo load and they left the camp together for the long haul up the Cwm followed by the steep climb up the Lhotse Face for Camp Three.

Many teams were on the move that day and the front

runners had kicked a path through the deep snow. Kami was thankful he wasn't breaking trail but the passage through the Cwm was still pretty tough and it took them five hours to get past Camp Two.

Four rope pitches followed on the Lhotse Face, the angle of the slope constant at about seventy degrees. Kami played the numbers game, counting out twenty steps before taking a rest. Every time he stopped to wait for Jamling he swigged on his water bottle, determined to keep himself hydrated at all costs.

A bunch of Sherpas passed them in the opposite direction, moving down swiftly after an equipment run up to the col. Jamling greeted many of them as they passed, accepting the gift of a cigarette and swapping news while Kami listened in.

'The summit ridge still isn't roped up,' he heard. 'Too much deep snow on the ridge.'

Jamling grunted at that.

'Same every year,' he said. 'It'll get done in the end.'

As soon as the cigarettes were finished the porters departed with haste, seeming to fly down the fixed ropes as they headed for Camp Two.

Jamling was slow to get moving again. The contact with the other group seemed to have demotivated him and he moved sluggishly up the trail, listlessly pulling himself up the ropes and hawking up phlegm in alarming quantities.

Kami recalled a comment by Brennan, 'Imagine seventy per cent of your lungs have been amputated … '

That really was how it felt.

He was curious to start using the oxygen but Tenzing had told them to hold off trying it until they reached the col.

'You go on ahead,' Jamling instructed. 'Make a platform for the tent.'

Kami was surprised. He had figured they would dig out the slope and put up the tent together. But Jamling said no more, just unwrapped another little plug of chewing tobacco and sat down for a further rest.

Kami kicked up the slope for another hundred vertical metres until he arrived at the Camp Three location.

He tied his pack carefully to a fixed line, assembled his snow shovel and chose a spot to start. A couple of friendly Sherpas resting in a nearby tent heard the sound of the spade and came out to help.

Just as the flysheet was pinned down in place, Jamling came into view fifty metres down the slope. Kami had never really thought of him as an old man but now he did look wasted.

'They'll flog him to death in the end,' one of the other

Sherpa's observed. 'We're like mules to these people.'

Kami thought about that as he watched Jamling climb slowly towards him.

Jamling was subdued that evening, and he showed no enthusiasm to help out with the chores.

There was little warning of the crisis to come.

O

In the middle of the night Kami woke with a start. He'd fallen asleep without knowing it. He turned on his head torch to check out Jamling's condition. His heart sank as the truth was so starkly revealed.

Jamling's lips were blue and his skin was a clammy shade of grey. Worse still, his breathing didn't sound right. His lungs were wheezing like an old bellows. Some kind of asthma maybe? Or something more serious?

Was it water on the lung?

Kami knew that a climber with altitude sickness could drown as liquid seeped into their lungs. No drugs could rectify the situation. The only hope was to get that climber down as fast as possible. Kami checked his watch. It was 3.a.m. Still four hours to dawn.

Could he risk waiting until first light?

He picked up the walkie talkie: 'Camp Three calling

Base Camp. Camp Three calling Base Camp.'

There was a silence which felt a hundred years long, then a voice blurted out loud and clear.

'Base Camp here. Is that you Kami?'

It was Tenzing. Dependable Tenzing manning the radios even at this unsociable hour. Kami rapidly explained the situation, describing Jamling's symptoms as best he could.

'You've got to get him down,' Tenzing told him. 'If he stays there he could be dead by morning.'

'I'm going to need some help.'

'OK. We'll alert Brennan and George. They're at Camp Two. We'll radio them now, get them to come up and help you down the Lhotse Face.'

'Right. Tell them to be fast.'

He unzipped the tent and was shocked to see how hostile the conditions were outside. In his preoccupation with Jamling he had hardly noticed that the blustery wind had strengthened into a storm.

'Wake up!' he shouted to Jamling. 'We've got to leave the tent.'

Jamling buried his head in the soft fabric of his sleeping bag, trying to escape the swirling vortex of snow that was circulating inside the tent.

Kami took direct action; he knew there was no time to lose.

He quit the tent, grabbed Jamling's boots and hauled him out on his back. It was a brutal way to treat him but he could think of no other way to do it. Then he took the sick man by the shoulders and hauled him up onto his feet.

The cutting blast of wind seemed to rouse Jamling out of his trance.

'Can't breathe properly,' he gasped. 'Need air.'

'You're sick. Put your arm around me,' Kami told him.

Jamling did as he was asked, resting his weight on Kami's shoulders as they moved slowly away from the tents and out onto the wind-scoured slopes of the Lhotse Face.

Supporting Jamling's weight was crushingly painful for Kami and he wondered how long he could bear it.

They navigated the route down to the rock steps, which were covered by a good metre of fresh powder. The deep snow here did them a favour; on the steeper sections Kami could get Jamling to sit down, sliding on his backside as Kami steadied him on a short rope. It was dodgy but it worked.

They made it to the big traverse, Jamling getting slower and slower, his head hunched deep into his Gore-Tex hood as he tried to escape the force of the wind and the biting sting of the snow granules.

'Keep moving,' Kami yelled.

Jamling eased his right leg forward a few inches. Then the left. He was moving like a zombie in a low-budget horror film, peering wide-eyed into the tempest with the mystified look of a man who has absolutely no idea where he is.

'Jamling! It's me! You have to wake up for me!'

Gradually, Jamling's eyes rolled back down; slowly, oh so slowly, they focused, that precious spark of recognition coming back again for a moment or two.

He nodded. Then sat down as he succumbed to a massive coughing fit. Kami waited a minute then cajoled the sick man back to his feet and they carried on down into the raging snowstorm.

What had happened to Brennan and George?

Kami was longing to see the flicker of head torches coming up.

What was taking them so long? Surely they should have reached them by now?

Jamling's breathing seemed to be getting worse, his cough ever more violent. When he spat onto the snow it was a frothy red/brown colour. Every twenty or so steps his legs would give way with frightening suddenness.

Had Brennan and the cameraman passed them somehow in the storm?

But he knew that was impossible; they would be coming

up the same fixed ropes that he was descending on. There was no way to miss them.

Two more hours passed and a lacklustre dawn sky finally glowed through the storm as Kami continued to coax Jamling down.

Finally, when the two of them were almost in sight of Camp Two, he saw the powerful figure of Brennan coming out of the white-out towards them. George was not far behind.

'You made it!' Brennan called out. 'Must have been a nightmare coming down the face!'

The sheer relief of reaching help was enough to fill Kami's eyes with tears and he lowered Jamling gently to the ice before collapsing by his side.

Moments later George was with them, already pulling the lens cap off his camera and flicking on the power. George framed up his shot and Brennan started his piece to camera.

'OK. We're out here on this horrific day. Blowing hard and plenty of snow. We made the decision to evacuate Jamling down to Base Camp but it's going to be touch and go now. Been a struggle to get him to this camp but we have to keep going now and make it to Camp One as fast as we can.'

Kami listened to Brennan's video piece with a growing feeling of confusion.

Brennan was making it sound like he had been in on the

rescue from the beginning. In reality the two Westerners had played no part in getting Jamling down the Lhotse Face. He hadn't even mentioned Kami's name, let alone given him credit for getting Jamling this far.

Kami didn't understand it at all but there was no time to dwell on it. They had to keep Jamling moving down or the day would end in disaster.

'He needs something to drink,' he reminded Brennan.

'Of course. We've got a flask here.'

George got a close up shot of Jamling as Brennan held a plastic cup of warm orange juice to his blistered lips. Then they re-filled the cup and handed it to Kami. The citric burst of sugar was a heavenly treat after the long hours of descent and he gulped down the liquid in seconds.

Brennan started to get Jamling upright and Kami scrambled up to help him. George didn't offer to help, but moved around them, forwards and back, taking a variety of shots of the rescue in progress as they moved slowly down the Cwm towards Camp One. Finally, Kami found the courage to speak up.

'What about George?' he asked. 'Can't he help us?'

'We really need him to keep filming,' Brennan replied testily. 'This is exactly the type of stuff the documentary needs.'

After that rebuke, Kami kept his mouth shut, and it

wasn't long before they saw a dark line of five climbers coming towards them. They were members of a Scandinavian expedition, a bunch of guys that Brennan had spent an evening partying with back at Base Camp.

As soon as they understood the situation they offered to help. Kami was finally able to take a break from the punishing physical labour as they completed the final two hours to Camp One. They got there at 2 p.m.

Word of Jamling's condition had spread amongst the teams at Base Camp and a dozen Sherpas had raced up through the icefall with a stretcher. Kami was told that a helicopter would be flying in to Base Camp later that afternoon to evacuate Jamling to Kathmandu.

Kami took his place at one corner of the stretcher, ready to do his part, but then he felt a firm hand on his shoulder.

'You're staying with us,' Brennan told him.

'But, sir ... ' Kami was taken completely by surprise. He hadn't thought for a moment that he would not be allowed to accompany Jamling down to Base Camp.

'We're going to need all the help we can get up here now,' Brennan continued.

'I will come back up tomorrow,' Kami promised.

'I can't risk it. You might not have the strength.'

'I will, sir,' Kami insisted. 'I can't leave Jamling alone.'

'He's not alone. He's got loads of people with him now. He'll be fine. You stay with us and that's the end of the story.'

Kami was gutted as he watched the rescue team move into the icefall. Every fibre of his being told him that he *should* be with Jamling all the way down. After all, what if Jamling woke up and asked for him?

For a crazy moment Kami wanted to run after them, to ignore Brennan's order and follow his heart.

But Brennan had overruled him and he was the boss.

Later he was taken to a tent and fed with lentils and rice. He drank cup after cup of hot chocolate and was loaned a sleeping bag by one of the other teams.

As he slipped into sleep his last thought was this; Nima gone. Jamling gone. What's going to happen next?

CHAPTER 9

George was already filming in the mess tent as Kami woke the next morning.

'You did a great job yesterday,' he told him, swinging the camera to get a close up of Kami. 'Maybe you even saved Jamling's life.'

'No problem,' Kami replied with a half smile. He still felt awkward and self-conscious when the lens was directed at him.

After breakfast Brennan outlined the plan for the day.

'We leave at eight,' he said. 'Non-stop up to Camp Three.'

George didn't look too impressed with this. 'Don't you think we should give everyone a rest day? Let the Sherpas come up through the icefall early tomorrow and then we all leave together?'

Kami silently applauded the plan. It made perfect sense. It would give his fellow porters a chance to recover down at Base Camp and he could use the day off himself.

'No,' Brennan was adamant. 'We lost a day yesterday bringing that old guy down. Now we need to make that time back.'

He followed this up with a terse radio call down to Base Camp, ordering the support team to leave right away. The response from Tenzing was less than enthusiastic – the Sherpas were still asleep at that moment.

'Wake them up,' Brennan replied. 'I need you to get those guys moving now.'

'Roger. Over and out.'

Brennan led the way that morning, breaking a trail through quite punishing soft snow. The Cwm was utterly silent save for the occasional clatter of rocks tumbling from the Nuptse Face.

Kami felt tired and listless as they got into the trek. Lunchtime came and went, celebrated with a brief stop for a muesli bar or two and a swig of Gatorade.

'Where are those guys?' Brennan kept repeating.

He was keeping a look out for the Sherpa support team which by now should have been cresting over the upper lip of the icefall.

He tried to raise Base Camp on the walkie talkie but, as was commonly the case in the Western Cwm, there was no direct line of sight and thus no signal.

One hour before Camp Two, the terrain started to rise up a ramp of rocky moraine. George slowed down dramatically, pausing often as coughing fits overcame him. Kami's skull began to pound with a forceful headache.

Brennan went ahead, going strongly and, if anything, putting on speed.

'He's a machine,' Sasha commented. 'How does he do it?'

Step by step they forged ahead, arriving at Camp Two by mid-afternoon to find Brennan waiting for them impatiently.

'I'm not feeling so great,' George told the boss. 'I'll never make it to Camp Three today. Why don't we do the sensible thing and hang on here for the night?'

'I second that,' Sasha agreed. 'We're all feeling it.'

'Kami could make it up there with me,' Brennan observed in a waspish tone. 'I could even train him how to operate the camera.'

The three of them stared up at the Lhotse Face, where Camp Three could clearly be seen some seven hundred metres above their position.

'What do you think, Kami?'

The young Sherpa wondered how to respond. He didn't want to say the wrong thing and offend the boss.

'I think it's better to rest here,' he ventured. 'Tomorrow we will be stronger.'

At that point George clutched at his guts, running behind a large boulder to answer an urgent call of nature.

'He's getting sicker,' Brennan said bitterly. 'He's shot hardly any footage today.'

There were a handful of Sherpas also at the camp, mostly working for a huge Japanese team. They received Kami warmly and invited him to their mess tent. He sipped a mug of yak butter tea but couldn't face the lentil stew they offered to go with it.

One of the Sherpas had a more powerful radio than the one that Brennan carried and Kami borrowed it to report back to Base.

'Tenzing? This is Kami. We made it to Camp Two.'

'Give me that thing.' Brennan had walked up behind him. Now he snatched the walkie talkie out of Kami's hands.

'What the hell's going on with the load carry?' Brennan demanded. 'I thought those Sherpas were coming back up through the icefall today!'

'They were out for fifteen hours yesterday,' Tenzing replied, an air of indignation entering his voice. 'Carrying

207

the stretcher down through the icefall has wiped them out.'

Brennan was gripping the walkie talkie so tightly his knuckles were white.

'What are you trying to tell me Tenzing? We *need* that oxygen.'

'They're completely exhausted, sir,' Tenzing insisted. 'You'll have to wait another twenty-four hours if you want those bottles.'

'I'll offer them a bonus. Fifty bucks apiece if they'll leave Base Camp right now.'

'Sir. It is not a question of bonus or no bonus. They don't have the strength to move out of their tents.'

Brennan terminated the radio call and tossed the walkie talkie into the corner of the tent.

'What's wrong with these people?' he raged. 'Where I come from you get paid for a job you do the job.'

'This is Everest,' Sasha reminded him gently.

'Sure. And those guys are Sherpas. This is where they belong.'

Kami wanted to intervene, to correct Brennan. Nobody *belongs* on Everest, he wanted to tell him. Not even the Sherpas.

At that moment the wind decided to come out and play, sending Kami running for the tent with the others. They ate an uninspiring meal, then, just before 9 p.m., they heard crampon spikes coming across the rocky moraine.

It was Norgay. The sole Sherpa to come up with more oxygen as Brennan had demanded. He had raced up through the icefall to Camp Two in just six hours, a phenomenal effort.

'I bring four bottles of O_2!' he exclaimed, collapsing exhausted into the tent and accepting a big mug of sweet tea.

'Nice work, Norgay,' Brennan congratulated him. 'You'll get your bonus for sure.'

Kami was delighted to have a fellow Sherpa with him. It took off some of the pressure and gave the two Westerners a big boost, even if the oxygen that had arrived was a fraction of what should have come up.

Norgay and Kami went to one of the other tents where they talked late into the night.

'It feels like the plan is going a bit wrong,' Kami observed thoughtfully. 'I thought the whole thing would be more … certain.'

Norgay laughed cynically. 'Certain? That's a good one. The only certain thing about this business is that there's no certainty at all. It's always a mess. Every time. There's too many things to go wrong.'

'How about Jamling?' Kami asked. 'Is there any news?'

'They got him to hospital,' Norgay told him. 'It's a good one in Kathmandu. If they can save him they will.'

Kami was happy to hear that Jamling was getting good care. He quietly said some prayers for him before he fell asleep.

O

The next morning was unusually calm; the mid-Asian jetstream had wandered off towards Mongolia for the day leaving Everest untroubled by even the faintest puff of wind. It was a rare moment and they all noticed it as soon as they quit the tent.

'This should be our summit day,' Brennan said with an air of regret. 'Not a breath of wind up there.'

'You think it'll stay like this for the next few days?' Sasha asked hopefully.

Norgay snorted derisively. 'No chance,' he said. 'Tomorrow will be business as usual. More wind. More storm.'

For the first hour of the morning, Kami enjoyed the peaceful sensation of climbing without the nagging wind. The mountain really was a different place without it and he settled into a steady rhythm, following Brennan up the fixed ropes.

Midway on the face they heard a clatter above.

Kami felt an adrenaline jolt as he saw black shapes tumbling down. For a terrible moment he thought they were bodies falling.

'Rocks!' Brennan cried out. 'Look out below!'

They dived for the ice, burying their heads in their arms as the boulders zipped past in a blur of speed and sound. Kami looked up, deftly rolling out of the firing line as he saw one the size of a basketball heading right for him.

It happened in an instant. Then it was over.

Just a few tens of kilos of smaller stones and grit pebble-dashing down the slope then an odd silence.

'You guys still alive?' Brennan called. They looked back down the slope, seeing with relief that all three of their comrades were still standing.

'Missed us by a whisker,' Sasha called up. Kami could hear the terror in her voice.

Kami scanned the slopes above them. The truth was that there were thousands of rocks perched up there. And many were far bigger than the handful that had just fallen.

They waited for the others to catch them up, sharing a drink and chatting nervously about the incident.

Kami felt jittery from that point on. The rockfall had been so sudden. The shock of it only really hit him about half an hour later as they continued the climb.

Any one of those falling stones could have killed them. It was pure luck that they had escaped injury.

They plugged on, reaching Camp Three in a state of paralysed exhaustion. For the next couple of hours they rested and rehydrated, then met at 8 p.m. in the dome tent to share the evening meal.

The boss was strangely silent as he picked at the pasta and sauce and Kami could tell he was building up to something.

Finally, when the plates had been cleared away he made an announcement.

'I've been thinking about our strategy … ' he said, 'and I've decided that Sasha should head back down.'

Sasha looked stunned.

'Head back down? To where?' she asked.

'Base Camp. I can't take the responsibility of you going any higher.'

Kami and Norgay caught each other's eye. They knew immediately that this surprising announcement could provoke the biggest row yet.

'I see. And on what basis is this decision made?' Sasha queried, fixing Alex with a flinty look.

'The rockfall made me reconsider your position,' Alex told her. 'Any one of us could have been killed in that incident. It reminded me what the stakes are here and I don't want you to get hurt.'

'I'm responsible for myself,' Sasha told him, a tinge of desperation clear in her voice, 'and the deal was I could go as high as I could manage.'

'You've done brilliantly. But enough is enough.'

'Don't patronise me! I'm all set for the summit and you know it.'

'Sasha ... I'm not patronising you, I'm just ... '

'I know what you're doing,' she retorted. 'You're finally succumbing to your own paranoia and removing me from the summit team in case I end up making you look bad.'

'No! That's not the ... '

The argument spiralled swiftly into a shouting match, with Sasha begging to be allowed to stay. Tears began to flow but Brennan was emphatic.

'I'm the leader of the expedition and my word is final.'

Sasha began to pull on her boots, tugging furiously at the knots. 'You only want one account of your great summit success and that's your own. Well, all I can say is good luck to you.'

And with that she ripped open the doorway and crunched across the ice to her tent.

Kami and Norgay cleared up the supper things and

bedded down for the night. They talked about the row as they played hand after hand of poker.

'She doesn't deserve to be sent back,' Kami said. 'It's not fair.'

'She would have summitted,' Norgay agreed. 'Maybe he doesn't want a woman up there with him?'

In the morning the atmosphere was even worse. Sasha nursed her tea with puffy red eyes and said nothing.

Alex had the weary expression of a man who hadn't slept at all.

Norgay was given the task of finding some Sherpas to escort Sasha down and, shortly after breakfast, he turned up with a couple of the Japanese team's men who were going to Base anyway and were happy to help out.

'Here you go guys,' Alex slipped them twenty dollars each and they nodded their thanks.

'You're getting good value for your money at least,' Sasha told him bitterly.

Kami, Norgay and George all got a tearful hug from the journalist.

'Good luck, guys. I know you're all going to do brilliantly up there.'

Then she started the descent, stepping carefully down the fixed line.

'That's done,' Alex told them without emotion. 'Now let's re-focus and keep going.'

The others packed up their things and the group of four swung out of the camp and began the tough ascent up to the col.

Kami was feeling pretty strong that day but he still felt stabbing pain in his calves and thighs. The snow from the storm had softened in the previous day's sunshine, making it difficult to walk through.

'Good day for an avalanche,' Norgay commented with some foreboding. Kami felt for the shrine bell in his pocket and said some hurried prayers for protection.

As it happened they did see an avalanche, but it was some distance away on the west side of the Lhotse Face and didn't threaten any of the climbers going up.

Seven long rope lengths followed, Kami counting off the changeovers in his head.

Ten pulls. Rest. Ten pulls. Rest. Breathe in hard. Trying to fill the lungs with air so thin it hardly seemed to exist.

They ate a couple of energy bars for lunch and sipped from a flask of tea. Far below them they could see the three tiny dots that were Sasha and her two companions. They were already halfway down the Western Cwm.

'Let's move,' Brennan told them. 'We don't want to be

arriving at the col in the dark.'

Then came the Geneva Spur, a long, undulating slope which seemed to go on for ever. False expectations kept cropping up and Kami often found himself thinking 'there's the top of the rise.'

But it wasn't. The gradient up this final stretch of the Lhotse Face was relentless right until the bitter end. Kami was taking a dozen breaths for every step of progress and even Brennan was struggling. But finally they front-pointed up a section of windslab and found themselves on the flatter terrain of the south col.

Kami took a good look around, impressed by what he saw. In his mind he had anticipated the flat area would be something the size of a football pitch. In fact it was many times larger.

Everest is always bigger than you can imagine, Kami thought.

They lay down for a rest, sharing a flask of hot spiced tea as they watched Norgay and the cameraman coming up that same punishing final section of the Lhotse Face.

'Now they're feeling it,' Brennan remarked with some relish.

At that moment Brennan's walkie talkie beeped into life and some unwelcome news came through.

A huge sérac had collapsed in the icefall. No one had been hurt but several ladders had been buried and the trail was closed for the next day or two while repairs could be made.

'We won't get that extra oxygen now,' Brennan announced gloomily to Kami and the others. 'We're really on our own.'

The four of them started out across the col, Brennan furious at the recent bad news, George so fatigued he was staggering as if he was drugged.

Kami could hear Brennan getting more and more irritated as they approached the area where the tents would be pitched. There were two dead climbers not far off, huddled figures which had been partly covered with small cairns of stones.

'We need a shot of those dead guys,' he kept saying. 'Why aren't you getting this?'

George did not respond, and showed no sign he had even registered the command.

'You want me to do it for you?' Brennan snapped finally.

The sarcastic tone seemed to wake George up. He roused himself enough to turn on the video, framing up a wide shot to record the impromptu graves.

As soon as the shots were completed the two Westerners threw off their rucksacks and collapsed onto the rocky surface of the col while Kami and Norgay put up the tents.

Brennan went across to the Japanese team to try and buy some oxygen to supplement the ten bottles his team had already stashed at the col. The answer was a firm 'no' which put the American into an even more poisonous mood.

There was not enough oxygen for all four of them to summit.

Brennan and George disappeared into their tent as soon as it was up. They took two oxygen cylinders with them and now Norgay pulled two more cylinders off the pile and Kami followed him into the tent.

'You tried this before?' he asked Kami.

'No.'

Kami placed the mask against his face and took an exploratory breath. He smiled as he felt the precious gas flooding into his lungs, amazed at the instant feeling of warmth that suffused through his body.

'Set it on one and a half litres,' Norgay told him. 'It'll last for hours like that.'

Kami clicked the gauge around as Norgay had told him, then lay back on his sleeping bag to rest. He knew Alex and George would be waiting for tea in the tent next door but he was just dead beat.

'Kami!' Brennan's roar shocked him out of his slumber. 'You got the cooker going?'

'Yes sir,' Kami called back.

While he waited for the ice to melt he noticed that his nose and cheeks were red raw with blisters. He had forgotten to put on his glacier cream that morning and later when he tried to sleep the pain just got worse. He tossed and turned all night, unable to find a comfortable position.

Only when he thought of Shreeya could he find a type of relief. He focused on happy memories of their time together, bathing at the village well in the warm air of the afternoon, watching the sun set from the high meadow.

In that way he managed to get a little sleep.

O

The next day was the first of their possible summit days but it seemed the wind hadn't read the schedule. A biting northerly blast was running hard on the summit ridge and the team made the prudent decision to rest for a day and do some filming if conditions improved.

At midday it slacked off a bit, allowing them to march across the col and do some filming on the ridge. Alex and Norgay formed a climbing pair, moving slowly up the ice band as George shot them from various angles.

Later he let Kami operate the camera for a few of the takes, giving him the freedom to choose the shots. It was thrilling to be in control of the kit and Kami loved it.

'You've got a natural eye,' George told him. Kami was pleased with the praise.

It was savagely cold. A few minutes standing still was enough to numb fingers and toes. George began to complain about his feet.

Alex did a piece to camera: 'We're in the death zone now. Well above eight thousand metres and it really feels extreme. My head feels weird, kind of like it's filled with candy floss. You can easily imagine how people just lie down in the snow and never get up again.'

Finally, they wrapped for the day, heading back for the tents. As they forged a trail back across the col George told Norgay 'my toes still feel weird.'

He stopped and stamped his foot, trying to get the circulation going.

'Not here,' Norgay told him. 'In the tent.'

Back in the camp the climbers lay resting for a while then wearily stripped off their crampons, harnesses and wind suits. It took them an age to perform these simple motions; commands from the brain were running at half speed and their hands floundered at the tasks.

'Let's see your feet, George,' Brennan said.

As George stripped off his two layers of boots there was

a collective groan. Three of the cameraman's toes were badly frostbitten, the tips bloated with puffy white blisters, the skin to the middle joint unnaturally waxy and grey. He touched them gingerly, examining them with the expression of a man who doesn't quite believe what he's seeing.

'That's it,' he said. 'I blew it.'

'Dead man's feet,' Norgay said with ghoulish relish. 'That's what we call them.'

'That's not helpful,' Brennan flashed Norgay an acid look.

'Does it hurt?' Kami asked sympathetically. The frostbite looked horribly similar to Nima's fingers.

'Not yet,' George told him, 'but I guess I'll have to thaw them out.'

'It doesn't look so bad,' Brennan said. 'Maybe you can carry on.'

'Not if I can't walk,' George pointed out with a catch in his voice. 'If I lose these toes I'll never climb again.'

'Bummer.' Brennan spat out the word, shaking his head in disbelief at this new stroke of bad fortune.

Norgay took hold of George's foot, examined it with an expert eye. 'They won't have to cut them,' he said finally, 'but your Everest is over.'

George tried to flex the toes, sucking in his breath as the pain began to strike. They brewed up some tea and drank it in silence, all four of them just staring at George's toes and figuring out what this would now change.

'I take you back to Camp Three now,' Norgay said quietly. 'Then Base Camp tomorrow.'

Kami thought Brennan might challenge this. Norgay was, after all, far more experienced than he was and might be more useful up high. But Brennan kept quiet and Kami remembered that the American had questioned the veteran Sherpa's motivation on more than one occasion.

Moreover, Kami knew how to operate the camera. That was probably the deciding factor, he thought.

George was close to tears. The pain was intense as his toes gradually thawed out and he was naturally freaking out at the thought he might lose them. The countdown to gangrene and putrefaction had started now and he knew that he had to get medical attention fast.

'I've let you down,' George told Alex. 'I figured I'd be good for the summit.'

'Don't blame yourself, man. We'll still get some shots,' Brennan told him, but the tone of disappointment in his voice was impossible to miss.

They exited the tent and Brennan and George embraced. George slapped Kami on the back.

'You're a good strong lad, Kami,' he said. 'You take care

up there and get some great shots, OK?'

'Yes, sir.'

'Go well, Alex,' George told the boss. 'I know you'll make it.'

'Thanks, buddy,' Brennan told him. 'Get yourself down to Kathmandu and save those toes, you hear?'

Norgay swung his pack onto his back and placed an arm around George.

'Let's go,' he said. Then they were off, two small figures lost on the vast plateau of the col. Kami watched them as they headed for the top of the fixed ropes which would guide them down the Lhotse Face, George giving him a final wave of the hand just before they limped from view.

It had all happened so quickly, Kami thought. One moment the mountain is benign, the summit within grasp. The next you are hurrying down with a condition that could leave you disabled for life.

'Looks like it's just the two of us,' Brennan said. 'We'll wake at midnight and leave as quickly as we can. And at least we'll have enough oxygen now.'

O

Those hours before departure seemed endless to Kami. He was trying to sleep with the oxygen mask on and finding it almost impossible. The fibreglass shell of the mask had eroded a blister on the bridge of his nose and it was horribly sore.

Brennan had slumped back onto his sleeping bag, utterly burned out by the filming session. The American's cough was persistent, he spat phlegm into a handkerchief and sucked on throat lozenges one after the other.

'Do me a favour Kami, can you brew up some tea?'

Kami flicked the lighter.

Brennan wriggled into his sleeping bag and wrapped himself up.

'Wake me up when it's ready,' he said, falling straight away into a profound sleep.

Kami, too, was longing to lie down. The desire to sleep was almost irresistible and Brennan's gentle snoring only made it more difficult to stay awake.

But he knew the importance of brewing up the tea, and he forced himself to watch the ice through drooping eyelids as it slowly, oh so slowly and reluctantly, yielded to the heat of the flame.

But finally it was done and he woke Brennan and handed him the steaming mug of tea. There was no sugar to be had here at the col so they both poured sachets of muesli into the liquid to sweeten it and give it substance.

Brennan slept for a couple more hours as Kami melted more ice. Then, just before midnight, Kami began to notice that the fabric of the tent was no longer flapping around. He unzipped the outer shell and poked his head out to take a look.

The clouds that had menaced the summit for the last three days were now gone.

It was perfectly still. Not a breath of wind.

'It's clear,' he told Brennan, shaking him awake. 'Take a look.'

'Cool. We're on.'

Then the dreaded process of getting dressed began – again. The struggle to climb into the down suit, arms and legs flailing in the tight confines of the tent; the swollen feet that had to be jammed into snug inner boots, the laces laboriously tied with traumatised hands.

When Kami emerged from the tent he found the night was brilliantly clear. An entire symphony of stars was playing across the heavens, so bright he could actually pick out the luminescence of their reflected glow on the ice beneath his feet. He reached up to the breast pocket of his wind suit, felt the precious shape of the little shrine bell there.

'Today,' he whispered, 'today if the gods allow.'

The Japanese climbers had left some time earlier; Kami

had heard them move past the tent. Now, on the lower section of the South-East Ridge, Kami could see three distant pin pricks of light moving up towards the balcony traverse. They were about two hundred vertical metres above the col, climbing slowly but steadily and the young Nepali envied their head start.

'Give me a hand with the crampons will you?' Brennan asked. Kami took off his gloves and kneeled in the opening of the tent to snap the metal spikes in place, threading the nylon strap through its double rings and pulling it back tight.

Brennan shuffled forward on his backside to exit the tent and accepted a helping hand from Kami to get to his feet. He slapped his hands together to encourage some circulation and shivered as the frigid night air sliced through his protective clothing.

'This is it, man,' he said. 'Do or die. We're not coming back without that summit.'

He raised his hand in a high five which Kami returned. The Nepali smiled but Brennan's words had struck him as hollow and the American's eyes did not have the same flash of light they had possessed earlier in the expedition.

'Let's do this!'

They turned on the regulator valves on their oxygen bottles and began to trudge across the col, Brennan leading the way slowly towards the ridge. Kami came after, his legs feeling weaker than he had ever known them. The five bottles of oxygen in his backpack seemed an unbearable weight during this first half-hour, but Kami knew the pain would ease as his muscles warmed up.

They began the slow grind up the ridge, gaining height at a rate of about sixty or seventy metres per hour. The route here was unroped and Brennan's progress was erratic. Kami was unable to get into a rhythm and after an hour of fitful climbing he was grateful when Brennan spoke.

'Can you take over in front?' he asked.

Kami did so, finding his natural pace and remembering Jamling's advice to keep his breathing under control. Brennan fell in behind him, matching the young Nepali's steady pace but still gulping for air and coughing intermittently into his oxygen mask.

Dawn was now just an hour away and Kami could sense the weather deteriorating. He gathered in the drawstring of his hood, pulling the down suit closer to his face to reduce the amount of exposed skin. But the wind still sliced through, making his cheeks numb and freezing the tip of his nose.

Daybreak was depressing. The light didn't erupt with a fanfare, it just sneaked up on the mountain and wrapped it in a sort of sullen grey shroud, a brooding pewter sky loaded with menacing clouds.

Kami felt his spirits sag. Was this a message from the gods, he wondered?

Brennan called a rest stop and Kami chipped out a small ledge with his ice axe so they could sit. Brennan unclipped his waist strap and shrugged off his rucksack. He opened it up and began to fiddle with the oxygen bottle inside.

'Problem?' Kami asked.

'Nah. Just some glitch in the airline.'

He closed up the rucksack and munched on a granola bar for a while. Then they got back up and continued the ascent of the ridge.

Kami focused on landmarks, wanting targets to head for. Mostly he set his sights on exposed rocks, counting out the laborious steps until he reached them. Once he set a mark on a patch of dark material some thirty metres above, only to find to his horror that it was the partly buried body of a dead climber.

They passed two more victims of the mountain in that hour alone, dessicated figures, their clothing ripped to rags by the wind.

At the place known as the South Summit – a small out-lying nodule of rock which was still a serious distance from the true top – they rested again and Kami was able to cache two of the full oxygen bottles for the return. Slipping the lighter pack on his back was a big morale booster; eight kilos less to carry.

More energy for the climb.

Every once in a while Kami had checked to see if he could see the Japanese team higher up the ridge. Earlier, the steepness of the terrain had obscured them from view.

Then he saw movement. Now the Japanese team were in sight above them, returning along the ridge. Kami tried to deduce from their movement if they had made it or not but at this distance there was no way of telling; they just looked like three immensely weary men.

Half an hour later, the first of the three man team arrived at their position.

'We made it!' The climber clasped Kami's hand and pumped it up and down in slow motion.

'That's great!' Kami told him with a huge smile as his two fellow climbers arrived.

'You get some good pictures?' Brennan asked.

'You bet. Video, phone call back to Tokyo, everything worked like a dream.'

The Japanese leader took off his goggles and polished off the ice which had formed across the lenses. He looked like a man who hadn't slept for a week, but the triumph of the summit was still burning in his eyes.

'How long to the top from here?' Brennan asked. His voice was becoming hoarse from the constant cough.

The Japanese leader looked back up the ridge.

'Three hours, maybe more.'

'Three *hours*?' Brennan and Kami exchanged a look. Neither of them believed it could possibly take that long from their position.

'I was watching you just now,' the Japanese leader continued, 'you're climbing too slow.'

'We'll make it,' Brennan told him.

'Maybe,' the leader replied, unconvinced, 'but you are too late my friend.' He tapped his wrist to emphasise that time was ticking away.

'Thanks for your opinion,' Brennan replied curtly, 'but I'll make my own decisions.'

'Whatever. I'm only trying to give you some advice.'

With that the three exhausted Japanese climbers picked up their ice axes and slowly resumed their descent.

'I need a good rest now,' Alex told him. He sat heavily on the ice, his head in his hands. He looked depressed, Kami thought, not surprising when considering how much work there was still to do.

Kami waited ten minutes. 'We go now sir?'

But Brennan did not respond. In fact, he seemed asleep behind his mirror goggles.

Kami had a sudden instinctive thought; he unclipped the straps on Brennan's rucksack and checked out the little red and green gauge on his oxygen cylinder.

It was showing empty.

Kami checked it again to be sure. It took a moment or two for his altitude-dulled mind to register what he was seeing but the information got through in the end.

Four litres a minute. The highest flow rate possible.

Brennan had set his delivery rate at the maximum.

No wonder his oxygen had run out so fast.

Jamling's words flashed into Kami's mind; strict instructions not to use more than two litres a minute maximum.

Brennan had ignored it.

All this was bad news, Kami knew, but there was something even more troubling; even though Brennan had been running on the maximum oxygen rate, he had been getting slower and slower as they headed up the ridge.

Brennan was really *suffering.* Altitude had undermined all that raw strength and corroded his ability to think straight.

What he had done was illogical and dangerous.

But what could Kami say? He could hardly reprimand the boss.

'I'm going to set up a new bottle for you,' Kami told Alex.

'Go for it,' Brennan mumbled.

Five minutes later it was done; the full bottle clipped onto the line and feeding into Brennan's mask at two litres a minute. Kami snapped the American's rucksack straps together and told him, 'All set.'

'That's a bit better,' Alex commented. He drew deeply on the oxygen, somewhat revived.

Kami pulled his fellow climber to his feet and they climbed around some rocky pinnacles and regained the ridge. Brennan was moving a bit better now he had more Os running into his system, but before long the epic climb entered a more technical phase.

A sheer wall some five metres high.

Kami realised it had to be the famous Hillary Step, the most serious technical challenge on the South-East Ridge.

CHAPTER 10

Kami stared up at the ice wall, feeling a surge of adrenaline course through his body. It looked serious and awkward in equal measure, patches of diamond-hard blue ice overlaid with wind-packed snow. Dozens of ancient ropes were embedded in the ice or just flapping uselessly in the wind.

This would be a real test, Kami realised, but he knew he could do it.

'You go first,' Brennan told him.

Kami could see a solid length of fresh rope had been fixed to the right of the climbing line. He pulled on it hard to test it then clamped his jumar onto the cord.

He started to climb, reaching up with his left arm to whack his ice axe into the face, gaining a bit of height then sliding the jumar clamp up the rope with his right hand.

After each upwards lunge, he kicked his crampon spikes into the ice surface and rested on his front points. Once or twice the snow crumbled without warning; giving way in an instant, leaving his legs scrambling in mid-air with all the weight on his arms until he could kick them back in to a firmer spot.

Kami's jumar/ice-axe combination wasn't the most elegant climbing technique but it was effective; after seven or eight moves he was able to lunge onto the shelf at the top of the Hillary Step. He flopped onto his stomach and lay there for long moments, savouring the satisfaction of the climb and trying to get his breath back.

'OK,' he called down to Brennan after a bit, 'your turn.'

Alex Brennan waved a hand at him but did not rise to his feet as Kami expected. Instead he just sat there staring out into the billowing clouds which now filled the Western Cwm, spindrift pattering against his wind suit, his shoulders hunched against the wind.

Kami left it for five minutes. Ten. He knew that things were getting really late now; they really *had* to get moving.

'You OK?'

'Yeah. Just taking a break,' Brennan shouted back.

A few minutes later Brennan got up and started the climb but he looked weak from the start. He wasn't *attacking* it as

Kami had done. Rather, he was pawing at the face, burning precious energy as he drew quantities of snow down.

But slowly he did manage to make some headway up the ice face, gaining two body lengths and reaching the mid-way point on the step.

Brennan reached up again with his ice axe, and plunged it into the face. But there was little power in the strike and the axe was not deep enough to get a true purchase.

Kami watched him struggling, amazed that this Olympic athlete could have been reduced to a shambling shadow of his former strength. He understood it; he was feeling the same effect in that moment – but the young Nepali knew he still had something left in the tank.

And Brennan was running on empty.

Finally, Kami made a decision. He reached down and grabbed hold of the back of Brennan's wind suit. He gritted his teeth and pulled up with a mighty heave, hauling his fellow climber up onto the snow shelf where they both now collapsed in a heap.

'That's a tough one,' Brennan gasped, 'thanks, man.'

They rested for a while, lying flat out on the ridge as Brennan coughed like his lungs were on fire.

Kami had no idea how much time went past as they waited in that exposed spot. Enough time for great regiments of clouds to sweep across the summit. It seemed that Brennan had given up looking at his watch.

Now the ridge was getting perilously narrow and the wind was coming in hard. Kami felt himself buffeted by the blast and he angled his body to prevent himself being blown off his feet, dropping his shoulder into the wind and standing side on.

While he waited for Brennan to catch him up, he stared ahead, realising with some despair that the summit still looked far away.

There was plenty of climbing still to go and all of it along that scary-looking ridge line.

Brennan was following on, but in fits and starts. He would take a few miniscule steps, then pause for what seemed to be an age, hunched over his ice axe and coughing with that deep lung-rattling shudder that had been worsening ever since Camp Two. Kami was itching to push ahead but he knew his duty and he would not leave the boss.

The walkie talkie squawked into life; Brennan fumbled for it in his pocket.

'We just lost you on the long lens,' Kurt told them. 'We got nothing but cloud here at Base, over.'

'We're still here,' Brennan replied. 'Still on the ridge and heading up.'

'We got a meteo report and it's not looking good,' Kurt continued. 'Wind's rising fast. The guys here are saying you should maybe call it a day.'

'Not now,' Brennan replied slowly. 'We've come too far to fail.'

Kurt started to reply but Brennan terminated the call. He clicked off the walkie talkie and stuffed it back into his pocket. Then he succumbed to another of the coughing fits and Kami couldn't help noticing flecks of blood in his saliva as he spat.

'You cool to keep going?' Brennan asked Kami.

'Yes, sir.'

A new gust of wind suddenly ripped across the ridge, sending them both crashing down for cover. Kami thrust the tip of his ice axe in as an anchor, holding on to Brennan's harness with his other hand as the violent blast threatened to blow them down the Kangshung Face.

The gust whipped away, taking a vast amount of ice particles with it. Kami got to his feet and surveyed the situation; he was shocked to find that none of the subsidiary peaks were now visible. Pumori, Ama Dablam, Changtse; all were smothered in cloud.

'We should keep moving, sir.'

No response.

Was he asleep? Or was cerebral oedema shutting down his brain?

Kami decided he would radio down to Base. The whole situation was way beyond his experience and he needed some advice from Tenzing or Lopsang. Should he try and persuade Brennan to turn around? Or was his condition more or less normal on a summit day attempt?

'Sir!' Kami gave the boss a gentle knock on the shoulder and he came around with a start. 'I want to use the walkie talkie sir.'

Brennan shook his head. 'No time for that. We've got climbing to do. Time is rolling on.' Brennan tried to rise, but slumped back. Kami clasped his hands, pulling him upright. He clipped both of their karabiners onto the frayed safety line, figuring that even doubtful protection was better than none.

Ten minutes' more rest. Brennan's flask giving them both a precious mouthful of sweet tea. Then back to the climb and the technical challenges of the ridge and the ever deteriorating weather.

Now Brennan was crawling more than walking. His breathing was definitely stressed. Kami could tell that every upwards movement required prodigious amounts of will.

How much longer could the American keep going? Kami was thinking about the dead bodies they had passed earlier.

The ridge became steeper again. Complicated rock requiring big steps up. Just what they didn't need, Kami thought miserably. Not vertical like the Hillary Step but not far off it. The American put his arm around Kami's shoulders, looking for support. But the terrain would not allow the two of them to pass in that way, the ridge was so narrow that only one could traverse at a time.

A further assault began from the wind, the force sufficient to make Kami wonder if his goggles would be ripped away from his face. Small stones and rocks were actually *moving* he realised as he stared downwards at his feet, prised out of the mountain's icy clutch and spun away down the Kangshung Face.

'Hell, Kami!' Brennan called out. 'We're so damn close! We can almost touch it from here.'

Brennan bent over as another feverish round of coughing set in. Kami didn't know what to say, unsure whether he should be encouraging the boss to go further or advising him to give the whole thing up and turn back for the col.

Brennan got himself upright, again with Kami's help. Over the next hour he made it about another ten metres along the ridge line, pulling himself along the fixed rope in a despairing manner which was devoid of conviction or strength. Every step cost him a five-minute rest.

Then he folded up. Just collapsed with nothing left to give, lying awkwardly with his thigh on a painful-looking rock. Kami helped him to shift into a better position, knowing in that moment, instinctively, that the summit quest was absolutely over.

And that Brennan knew it too.

'You know what makes me more sad than anything?' the boss rasped.

'No sir.'

'All the people who've put so much into this. People back home, people down at Base. It's not just for me, this whole thing, you do know that don't you?'

The clouds had darkened. Kami sensed the wind was intensifying again, that a full-on storm was now brewing to the north. He flexed his fingers inside his gloves wondering if they were really as frozen as they felt.

'I think I understand, sir.'

'Hell, we're pretty much on the summit anyway.'

No we are not, thought Kami. We are still very far from the summit. Far enough that you will not make it.

Kami's hand moved to the shrine bell where it sat nestled safely in his breast pocket. He looked up the ridge line, longing for the freedom to leave Brennan and complete the promise he had made to Shreeya.

To put the shrine bell in the true home of the gods. The real summit of the world.

He knew that he had the strength to make it. There was no question of that. A half-hour more of effort would get Kami to that sacred spot. He could scrape a little hole in the ice and place the shrine bell reverently inside before covering it up. The sins of the past would be forgiven and he could return to Shreeya with his head held high.

But abandoning the American would be a cardinal sin. The boss was already disorientated and confused. He needed Kami with him and there was no getting around that.

'They don't deserve us to fail, Kami,' Brennan said. 'We owe it to them … even if we have to … ' his words tailed away as fresh snow began to be driven through the air.

'What did you say, sir? I am sorry I could not hear you,' Kami bent down closer.

Brennan was hit by more coughing. Each attack seemed to be deeper, inflict more pain.

'Maybe we can still make give this some kind of happy ending? You know what I'm saying?'

'I don't understand, sir. I am sorry. We have to turn around now.'

'What do you say we make this the summit?'

Brennan's desperate, bloodshot eyes burned into Kami.

The young Sherpa did not know where to look.

'Take a photo or two … make it seem … '

It was an excruciating moment and he wasn't entirely sure he really understood Brennan's intention. Was he proposing to pretend they had reached the top? That was how it seemed.

Kami was utterly lost. What should he do? How should he act?

'Everything is your decision, sir,' he said. It was the only thing he could say.

'There'll be an extra bonus for this,' Brennan told him. 'But you'll have to back me all the way.'

Kami remained silent. He was bewildered by the unexpected direction the conversation had taken.

'Will you back me all the way Kami?'

Kami nodded uncertainly. 'Of course, sir, that is my job.'

Brennan handed Kami his digital camera.

'Get a good shot,' Brennan said. 'Make sure you get me in the middle of the picture, right?'

'Yes, sir.'

Close to their position was a prominent fang of rock and ice. Brennan crawled over to it and managed – with some considerable difficulty – to get himself upright. He struck a weary but victorious pose with his ice axe in the air, the wind and snow raging about him.

'Take a few,' he told Kami, 'might as well get a good one.'

Kami clicked away. Brennan checked the images and tucked the camera back in his pocket. At that moment the walkie talkie ripped out a bleep; it was Kurt.

'Base Camp to summit team. Base Camp to summit. You guys are scaring us now. Please God tell us you're on the top of the world.'

Brennan thought for a few moments then replied, 'We're here. Job done.'

'You say job done! You're on the summit … ?' Kurt's voice was filled with instant joy.

Kami watched Brennan closely. The American turned his face away …

'We just kept going … just kept moving and fighting and Kami's been a star, man, he's kept me going all the way.'

'They made it! They made it!' Jubilant cheers broke out thinly from the walkie talkie. 'Congratulations Alex and well done Kami you two are amazing do you hear me amazing! This is just so cool.'

'It's all down to Kami,' Brennan replied. 'I wouldn't have had the strength myself.'

'You're a force of nature, Alex. The world is yours from now on, you know that don't you?'

There was a brief pause, then a Sherpa voice came on. It was Tenzing. 'Kami? The gods are smiling on you!' he said. 'You've done us proud and you'll be a great Everest man! This is the first of many, many ascents to the top.'

Kami wanted to take the walkie talkie but Brennan didn't offer him the handset. Instead he asked 'Have you got the radio link lined up?'

'You bet we have,' Kurt responded. 'Hold the line.'

Brennan was connected to an interviewer at an American radio station. Kami heard him describe the climb, the weather, the pain, the joy of taking those few final steps onto the top of the world … As the chat droned on, Kami felt his eyes drawn irresistibly up the ridge. To the *real* abode of the gods. How long would the interview last? Could he steal away and place the shrine bell there while Brennan was …

Too late.

'I feel this is a gift from God,' Alex concluded. 'We've been blessed to reach this place.'

Kami noticed something unusual. Two narrow filaments of ice were growing out of the lower plastic rim of the boss's goggles.

He was crying. Those thin rivulets of ice were actually frozen tears.

'One last question, sir. Are you ready for the Primaries?

244

Do you think you can win the nomination?'

Brennan's piercing eyes were invisible behind the mirror glass.

'Well they say every great journey begins with a single step. Maybe I just took that step here on the summit of Everest.'

'And a final word?'

'God bless America. I'm on my way home.'

The interviewer signed off and Kurt came back on to conclude the radio link.

'You have to come back safe now! Remember you're only halfway there!'

'We got that. Over and out.'

Brennan clicked off the walkie talkie and stood staring out into the clouds. His head suddenly flopped forward, as if all the tendons in his neck had just been severed. He put his weight onto his axe, half falling before Kami caught him.

'I'm so tired, Kami,' he muttered. 'I hardly ... '

He wanted to sit but Kami wouldn't let him. 'No more rest, sir. Now we have to get back to camp.'

The retreat began, hauling themselves back down the ridge line, picking footfalls with infinite care, praying that the fixed lines would hold as the wind continued to rip across the peak.

Kami had Jamling's warnings in his mind. 'Coming down more dangerous,' Jamling had said time after time. 'Seventy per cent of people die coming down.'

Kami kept that in his mind, ultra-aware that he was responsible not just for his own safety but that of his fellow climber as well.

Just above the Hillary Step, Kami turned for one last view of the summit ridge. He had the crazy urge to shout 'I'm sorry' to the gods. Sorry that he had got so close and had not given them the devotion that they deserved. Sorry that he had failed to place Shreeya's tribute in their safe keeping.

Sorry also that he had failed to get Brennan to the top.

But a dense cloud had claimed the mountain. The ridge was all but lost to view and he could not bring himself to cry out as he wanted, knowing that Brennan would fail to understand.

Besides there was still so much to do.

Kami now had the responsibility of getting Alex Brennan back to safety. The boss's life was in his hands and there was a long, long way to go.

O

Three days later, Alex Brennan and Kami made it back to Base Camp. The mountain had stamped its mark; they stumbled with zombie steps, faces seared by ultraviolet assault, bloodshot eyes dulled with the impact of extreme physical exhaustion.

Kami couldn't believe how drained his body felt. Not even on the most punishing tree-cutting days with his father had he experienced anything like this bone-crunching fatigue. Every sinew in his body felt like it had been given the work-out from hell.

A welcoming party was waiting for them impatiently at the foot of the icefall. Twenty members of the expedition – Westerners and Sherpas alike – were there to clap and cheer them out of the last danger zone.

'You made it! You made it!' Sasha was bouncing up and down with joy, hugging first Alex, then Kami, as cameras flashed off on all sides.

'Respect!' Kurt told them both earnestly. 'I'm in awe of your achievement. And jealous as hell!'

Kami found himself cracking up into tears. The goodwill flooding over them was so genuine, the clamour so packed with emotion that he couldn't prevent it.

'Take this,' Sasha gave Kami a tissue and he dabbed at his eyes.

The young Sherpa felt an alien sensation overwhelming him; the glorious feeling of being safe. That the dangers were over. That the mountain couldn't touch them any more.

'I had a bet you were going to make it!' Lopsang told him, his eyes sparkling with pleasure. 'Tenzing owes me a hundred rupees!'

For Kami it was a sheer delight to see the faces of his fellow Sherpas. They jostled round him, slapping him on the back, embracing him extravagantly and asking a thousand questions at once.

'Any frostbite? Bits fallen off?'

More than anything he wished that Jamling and Nima could have been there. And Shreeya of course.

'Get the packs off,' Kurt ordered. 'Come and celebrate the proper way.'

The two climbers shrugged off their rucksacks, allowing themselves to be hustled over to the mess tent by the jubilant team.

'There's a shower waiting for you two guys when you're ready,' Sasha teased them.

'Are you trying to tell us we stink?' Brennan laughed.

'Well ... ' A well-aimed toilet roll hit her on the shoulder.

Plates of Sherpa stew were placed in front of the two men. They both fell on the food, spooning it down quickly, ravenous for the calories after days of surviving on muesli bars and hi-energy drinks.

'Let me see the papers,' Alex demanded. 'Did we get

plenty of coverage?'

'Did we ever?' Sasha told him with an impish grin. 'Your face is all over them like a rash.'

A laptop was quickly fetched and Alex began to scan the pages of the online editions, his face creasing with pleasure as he saw the sheer amount of coverage.

'Check this out, Kami,' he said, pulling him to his side so he could see the laptop screen.

Sasha had been super busy, emailing out copy and pictures to all the main press agencies. Brennan had been able to borrow the Japanese team's satellite module at the col, sending the 'summit' shots instantly back to Base so no time had been lost.

The result was a resounding media victory for Brennan. *The New York Times* had run the summit shot across half of the front page with the banner headline,

TODAY – EVEREST: TOMORROW – THE WHITE HOUSE?

Beneath the picture was a positive thousand-word article outlining Brennan's political views and hopes for reform at the highest level. The report ended:

> Alex Brennan's triumphant ascent of Everest reveals a core of steel and a single-minded focus that will serve him well on the forthcoming presidential campaign. If he can connect with the people he could go (once more) all the way to the top.

Virtually all of the newspapers had used Kami's shot of Brennan, the raised ice axe signifying victory, his weary, ice-burned face split by a summit-sized grin. There was no doubt it was an iconic image, loaded with power and personality.

But it was not what it seemed. And Kami couldn't forget that.

Of course, everyone had believed the photo was taken on the true summit.

But it made him feel like he was an accomplice to a trick, a fraud. It was a feeling that had been growing inside him during the descent; one of ever-more regret that they had not been able to push for that final section of the climb.

The shame of not getting Shreeya's shrine bell to the top.

Kami felt a gentle tug at his sleeve.

'Come to the shrine,' Tenzing urged him, 'before you forget.'

Kami made his excuses to the Westerners, slipped his boot inners on and followed Tenzing out onto the glacier. Suddenly he remembered. 'How about Nima? And Jamling? Have you got any news?'

'Nothing on either,' Lahkpa replied with regret. 'Nima seems to have vanished. Jamling is still in the hospital.'

Kami mulled on this slightly depressing news as they walked over to the chorten and performed a small cere-mony of thanks.

He mumbled some improvised words to praise the gods for their care, but he felt hollow inside. He should have been rejoicing, but in a very real sense the climb had not been completed. A tiny piece of the story was missing and he felt sure that the gods must know that.

And surely, he thought, it would trouble them as it did him?

They returned to the tent where the team were looking at a laptop, viewing the still pictures from the climb.

'What about your summit shot Kami?' Sasha asked.

'Yeah,' Tenzing agreed. 'I want to see it too.'

'Ah ... well ... mmm ... ' Kami's mind floundered for a response but he simply didn't know what to say.

He heard Brennan cough loudly as the mess tent quietened down.

He risked a swift look at Brennan, wanting his help, but all he saw in those bloodshot eyes was a glint of silent warning. He felt a ripple of panic in his belly; neither of them had thought that anyone would raise this question of Kami's summit shot.

'It's OK ... ' Kami muttered, 'I didn't go there to get a photo ... there are more important things.'

Brennan leaned across the table and slid the laptop back towards him.

'I hold my hands up on that one,' he said, 'with the

excitement of the radio call and all that I must have forgotten.'

'You forgot it? You didn't get a summit shot of Kami?' Sasha said, outraged. 'He risked his life to get you there and you couldn't spare a hundredth of a second to point the camera in his direction?'

'We didn't have a lot of time … ' Kami said, painfully aware of how unconvincing his voice sounded.

'OK,' Sasha continued, 'but it still sucks … '

Tenzing dragged the laptop out of Brennan's grasp and clicked back to Brennan's summit shot.

'Anyway you did a bad job of this one,' he said accusingly to Kami. 'No summit pole. No summit flags.'

Some of the other Sherpas clustered in to see, murmuring with agreement as they too noticed the missing details of the shot.

'That's true,' Lopsang said to Kami. 'You should have got him next to the summit pole.'

'Give the guy a break will you?' Brennan snapped. 'He's hardly used a camera before.'

He flipped down the lid of the laptop and stuffed it in its carrying bag. A sticky, uncomfortable few moments followed as the irritable exchange hung in the air.

'Anyway!' Kurt broke the spell. 'We got the coverage we

need and there's plenty more interviews to come.'

'To Kami!' Brennan accepted a glass of whisky and raised it for a toast, 'he was a real hero up there.'

The room erupted in a cheer for Kami as he felt his head start to spin.

'Drink! Drink!' Someone pressed a celebratory mug of beer into Kami's hand but he felt so wiped out he knew he couldn't face it.

Lopsang and Tenzing helped him to one of the tents and he abandoned himself to the deepest sleep of his life.

O

After seventeen hours dead to the world, Kami was up and about. It was not long after dawn and his head was pulsing with a savage headache. He had to gulp down litres of water to quench his thirst.

Kami didn't get any sympathy. In fact, to his amazement, the first thing he was told by Tenzing when he entered the mess tent for some tea was that he was expected to join four of the other Sherpas on a trip up to Camp Three.

Back on the mountain. Back up high.

'We need to dismantle the camps. Bring down the tents and all the gear,' Tenzing told him.

'But ...' Kami was gutted to get the instruction. He craved

rest as he had never craved it before and it all seemed totally unfair. Wasn't there some special time out for those who had been to the summit?

He bit his tongue. But Tenzing couldn't help notice the flash of anger that crossed his face.

Something else rankled Kami as he ate some porridge for breakfast; Alex Brennan certainly wouldn't be going back up again through the dangerous icefall to retrieve the kit. Instead he would be taking it easy down here at Base, luxuriating in the yurt and doing more of the endless radio and TV interviews which had been scheduled.

Where was the justice in that?

Kami wanted to launch some bitter words at Tenzing. He had done so much. Given everything. And still he had to give more.

'I know it's tough,' Tenzing told him with some sympathy. 'That's the way it has to be.'

And so began a further forty-eight-hour Sherpa raid on Everest, the clear-up operation that Kami had never anticipated. Not only was he physically at his weakest, but his mind was churning with resentment at having to do this final task.

They stayed a night at Camp One, then headed up for Three. The trail up through the Cwm was a real slog;

deep monsoon snow sapping their strength. But finally they reached Camp Three and stripped it down. Every last tent peg, sleeping bag and snow stake was packed away, and they descended with monster loads to Camp Two where they slept through the night before finally returning to Base.

Kami took a cold-water shower, ate a huge meal of corned beef and potatoes then went to his tent. He wasn't in the mood to see anyone but not long after, looking strangely ill at ease, Brennan came to see him.

'Just to show you I'm as good as my word,' Brennan told him.

He slipped a blue airmail envelope out of his pocket and handed it to Kami.

'Thank you.'

Kami placed the envelope in his lap, hardly daring to touch it, like it was a religious offering, or a wounded bird.

'Don't you want to open it?' the American asked.

Kami opened up the envelope with trembling hands. Inside was a thick wad of dollar bills.

'Count it,' Brennan ordered.

Kami plucked out the money and counted it out onto his sleeping bag. The cash had that enticing, sharp, musty and metallic smell of brand-new notes. Each of the fifty-dollar bills was crisp and clean, he noticed, so unlike Nepali rupee notes which were invariably scuffed or torn.

He put five hundred in a pile, then made another. That was now one thousand dollars and he stopped at that point and looked questioningly at Brennan.

'I thought about what you did up there,' Brennan shrugged. 'I figure you deserve more.'

Two more piles stacked up before Kami was done.

'Two thousand dollars should put a smile on your face,' Brennan said.

'Yes, sir. Thank you very much.'

'I just don't want you to be ... disappointed about the way things worked out,' Brennan said, hesitantly.

Kami hung his head. He knew exactly what Brennan was talking about.

'And ... I wanted to be sure that you were happy.'

'I am happy, sir. Really.'

Kami picked up his wallet to place the money inside; as he did so a few items fell out onto the sleeping bag – his identity card, a folded letter from Shreeya – and the business card the journalist had given him at Namche.

Brennan was on it in a flash.

'What's this?' he asked. He examined the card closely, the blood running out of his face. 'Why have you got this?'

'Erm ... well. You see ... '

'I don't see, Kami!' Brennan's anger rose in a flash. 'Please tell me you're not thinking about contacting this man. Not after everything that happened with Nima and Pemba.'

'No, sir, that would never happen ... '

'Has he offered you money? For bad stories about me?'

Kami was silent.

'This man is a scumbag, Kami. He writes lies and destroys people's lives. I want you to promise me that you will never, ever contact him.'

'I promise. I promise.'

'And you mustn't talk to Sasha either. Not about me and specially about ... about you know what.'

'I understand. Really.'

'I hope so, Kami. I really do.'

Brennan put the card in his pocket and quit the tent.

Kami was shaken by the attack of rage and paranoia and it took him some time to recover.

But then he got to thinking about the money and he took it back out to stare at it again, wondering if he was dreaming this moment. Two thousand US dollars! A quick visit to one of the money changers in Namche Bazaar would convert it into more than twenty thousand rupees, a king's ransom in Nepal. Kami had rarely had possession of more than fifty rupees in his life so this instant fortune was almost terrifying in its scale.

But what it represented was something beyond price; with this bonus Kami could buy himself out of the marriage contract with Laxmi. The money meant a future with Shreeya was now possible. He stared at the clutch of bank notes, thinking how bizarre it was that a stack of paper could mean so much.

His mind turned to Shreeya and he felt the tender glow he always felt when he thought of her.

Then, turning the little shrine bell over in his hands, he was seized with a terrible surge of guilt.

How was he to explain to her that he still had the bell? He had sworn on the gods that he would never tell a soul that they had faked those summit shots, so what excuse could he come up with when she realised he still carried her gift?

A new idea struck him. He could throw the bell away, drop it off one of the suspension bridges into the Dudh Kosi river. But the bell was an integral part of the puja ceremony, a holy object. Discarding it in such bad faith would be an open invitation to bad fortune. The gods are ever watchful, Kami knew, and they would not let such a provocation go unpunished.

Next morning Kami begged paper and pen from Sasha.

He wrote a letter to Laxmi's father, explaining that he was now in a position to pay back the dowry three times over as the man had demanded.

'Please send me back a message to say that you accept the money,' he concluded, 'and that the marriage contract is now over.'

He sealed up the money and letter in an envelope and sought out one of the expedition's two mail runners. Unencumbered by large packs, these fleet-footed athletes could cover in one day what would take an ordinary person four long days of toil.

Kami's package would be in Laxmi's father's hands within a matter of days. With luck, he would have a reply within the week.

Watching the mail runner set off down the glacier was an emotional experience for Kami and a whole bunch of fears and second thoughts assailed him. What if the man was robbed by bandits? An accident could befall him. He might tumble off a path and die in a ravine.

There was so much at stake.

He could have held onto the money, of course, waited a couple of weeks until the end of the expedition and sorted things out then. But he didn't want to wait. He feared his own conscience too much. If he got another attack of guilt like the previous night he might succumb to the urge to give the money back to Brennan, and then where would he be?

Back at square one, doomed to marry a girl he didn't love.

A pair of dark black ravens followed the runner as he loped away from Base Camp, sparring and dueling just a few metres above his head.

Kami hoped that was not a bad omen.

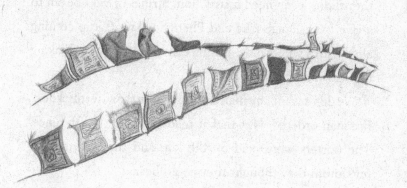

CHAPTER 11

The following day marked the beginning of the final stage of the great expedition; the dismantling of Base Camp and retreat back down the valley to Lukla.

Just eight days remained before the Westerners would fly out to Kathmandu.

The entire team set to it with great urgency. They had been up high for more than eight weeks and the desire to get out of Base Camp was universal. It had been eight weeks without family contact. Eight weeks on the unpalatable expedition diet. Eight weeks breathing in thin, cold, gritty air that left the human body unsatisfied with every breath.

No wonder everyone was desperate to escape.

Most of the Sherpas had been through this before and

they didn't even need instruction. Strings of yaks began to arrive from Dingboche and Pheriche, Base Camp coming alive with a whole new shifting community of wild-looking herders and porters.

'We don't want any man carrying more than twenty kilos,' Brennan ordered. Not that it made a shred of difference. The porters were paid by the kilo and they carried the maximum they thought they could bear.

They laughed at the Westerners who voiced sympathy for their plight. As far as they were concerned it was every man for himself and the more money to be made the better.

At last it was done. The expedition was packed up and ready to roll. All that was left on the glacier to show they'd ever been there were the raised tent platforms, now strangely deformed, the puja cairn with its wind-tattered prayer flags and the clouds of crows which fought for scraps of food.

Kami was happy to see the back of the place. Every step from now on would take him closer to a reunion with Shreeya. He took the glacier trek in his stride, feeling strong on the seven-hour descent.

On the first night of the pull out the expedition reached the yak herders' settlement at Gorak Shep. Kami was unloading his yaks when he suddenly felt a hand on his shoulder.

'I got some news for you,' Tenzing told him with a beaming smile. 'Jamling's doing all right.'

Kami felt a wave of relief wash over him.

'He's alive?'

'Yeah, we got an email from Kathmandu this morning,' he replied. 'He's through the worst of it, sitting up and eating like a pig if I know him.'

Kami laughed out loud at the thought.

'It was fluid on the lung,' Tenzing continued, matter of fact. 'You were right to bring him down, it's been touch and go.'

'When will they let him out?'

'Soon. A few days' more recovery and that'll be it. They'll put him on a flight into Lukla.'

Lukla! The expedition would be there in five days, Kami knew. If all went well he could be reunited with Jamling before the week was out. It was a wonderful thought.

The news of Jamling's successful recovery gave Kami a huge boost.

Jamling was better! Alive and well. The good news about his mentor seemed to put everything in a new perspective and Kami felt himself re-energised both physically and psychologically as the team continued the journey out of the highlands.

Over the following two days the expedition finally left

the world of rock and ice and re-entered a richer domain of vegetation, flowers and crops.

For two months they had been living in an environment with an incredibly limited range of smells. Now they delighted in the rich aromas of these lower altitude pastures; in the perfume of edelweiss and oleander, the delicate, loamy scent of earth, and the homely smell of baking chapattis leaking from the kitchens of the yak herders huts.

'Grass! I never thought I'd get off on the smell of grass!' Sasha said with a ringing peal of laughter, sniffing the ground theatrically at the lunch stop and playing the clown.

Then it was back on the trail, the sentinel peak of Ama Dablam becoming visible for the first time as they passed through the gated barrier of the Sagarmatha National Park.

Tenzing called a halt to the trek just after 4 p.m. that day and the camp was erected as usual.

Kami was kept busy; Lopsang had him peel a mound of potatoes and then he was sent to buy some firewood and eggs. Finally, as darkness fell over the camp, Tenzing asked him to take two jerrycans down to the river to fill up with water. Kami did as he was asked and, by chance, his path back through camp took him past Sasha's tent.

As he walked alongside it she called to him.

'Hey, Kami, how's it going with you?'

Kami came to the opening of the tent.

'I'm OK,' he told her.

'Come on in,' she told him. 'But take your boots off.'

Kami unlaced his boots and left them in the foyer. Then he manoeuvred himself into the tent, sitting next to her on the soft surface of a sleeping bag. The tent was filled with a gentle glow and he saw that she had lit a night light and placed it in a glass holder.

'I love candles,' she told him. 'They make me calm.'

Sasha brought out a Thermos flask.

'Would you like some tea?'

Kami nodded and she filled a plastic mug with the sweet fluid.

'I heard about Jamling,' she continued, 'sounds like he's going to pull through fine.'

'Yes. Really good news,' Kami replied as he sipped the delicious tea. 'He's a great man.'

'I hope it cheered you up. You've been looking pretty miserable for a guy that just summitted Everest.'

Kami felt his guts turn over. It made him nervous to think he could be read so easily.

'Lots of things on my mind,' he told her.

'Want to share them with me?' she asked casually. 'You know you can talk to me as a friend.'

'I don't know … ' Kami stammered, 'Maybe now is not the moment.'

'Why not? I just sense this deep unhappiness in you, Kami, and I really think it would do you good just to talk to someone.'

Kami took a deep breath. Was this the moment? Was it right that he pour out his problems to this American girl? He felt an overbearing desire to spill out his miseries and fears.

But before he could start to talk he heard footsteps crunching across the frosted grass and he knew it would be Brennan before he even looked out of the front of the tent.

'Knock knock,' the boss said. He kneeled in front of the tent and handed Sasha a small box. 'Returning your headphones.'

'Thanks.'

Kami guessed that Alex had spotted him slipping into Sasha's tent. Returning the headphones was just a ruse to see what was happening.

'I'll see you later,' Kami told Sasha. He slipped on his boots.

'Oh, OK.'

Kami walked across the field towards the mess tent but Brennan was waiting for him. 'What's going on between you and Sasha?' he snapped.

Brennan's head torch was shining right into Kami's face but he made no effort to switch it off. Behind that blazing beam Kami could feel the American's eyes boring into him in the most intrusive way.

'What do you mean?' Kami managed to stammer. He felt his face flush scarlet.

'I don't know. You tell me,' Brennan continued brusquely. 'Just thought there was an ... atmosphere between you two in that tent.'

'No, sir. Not at all.'

'Don't humour me!' Brennan hissed, suddenly more openly angry than Kami had seen him. 'I've seen the weird way she looks at you.'

'She's friendly to me,' Kami muttered, 'that's all.'

'What does she want from you, Kami? That's what I don't understand.'

'Nothing, sir. Just talking.'

Brennan leaned in close to Kami. His words were measured, packing serious punch;

'One thing you have to understand,' he told Kami slowly, as if talking to an imbecile, 'anything you tell her will appear on the front page of a newspaper in the United States within twenty-four hours. You might think you can tell her things in confidence but that would be the biggest mistake of your life, Kami. You cannot trust her for a single second.'

'But … '

'You must not talk to her about what happened on the summit ridge. Not one word. Not even if she swears that it's just a conversation between two friends. Is that clear?'

'Yes, sir.'

'I'm disappointed,' Brennan continued, 'I thought I could trust her but now I'm not so sure.'

'Don't say bad things about her!' Kami hissed. 'Please! I don't want to hear this any more.'

Kami turned and ran blindly out of the camp, heading for the Dudh Kosi river. At the banks he paced back and forth, half wanting to go back and tell Sasha everything, half wanting to run and run through the night until he reached his village and Shreeya's embrace.

Confusion and mixed emotions buzzed in his head. He wanted to be loyal to Alex. But at the same time he wanted the truth to come out. He walked up and down the riverbank in a daze, hardly caring where he ended up, lost in a miserable world of his own.

When the bell went for supper Kami decided to skip it.

The last thing he wanted to do was sit in that claustro-phobic tent with its secrets and atmospheres and Brennan's constant stare.

It was more than he could bear.

O

The retreat continued, down past the village of Pangboche and then onto the steep zigzag trail for the five-hour trek to Khumjung. The pace was slowed by continuous snow, the track churned up into a muddy mush which drained the yaks of all their strength and filled the climbers' boots with freezing slush.

Then a message arrived for Kami – the mail runner had returned from his village and had a letter for him.

He ripped it open with trembling fingers, scarcely daring to read it.

It was short and absolutely to the point.

> Kami,
> *I accept the money and absolve you of the marriage pact.*
> Chandra

Kami's heart thumped with joy to read those simple words. The one-line letter represented a whole new life for him and Shreeya.

He had done it.

They were free! After all the years of stress, of longing and

*frustration it had finally happened – the marriage pact was
over and the future was theirs to decide.*

A great wave of euphoria ran through him; he wanted to
run and jump, to shout the news from the rooftops, to tell
each and every one of the Sherpas about this great thing
that had happened.

But he was shy to do it, so instead he ran through the
village and made his way to the shrine that sat outside the
local monastery.

He had to sweep snow off the top to begin the devotion
but soon he was chanting a series of prayers to just about
every god he could think of. The words tumbled out of
him, a string of mantras honouring the great powers.

As the prayers ended, he took the shrine bell from his
pocket, intending to ring it to end the puja.

But, as he held the tiny bell in his hands, a curious feeling
of melancholy overwhelmed him and he hesitated to ring it.

*Suddenly his mood crashed; he felt small and lost. He still
had not resolved that big question. How to tell Shreeya that he
had NOT placed the bell on the summit.*

Would she understand? Probably yes, he decided. But
that was not the end of the issue; it was the GODS who
had to accept the story and Kami was not at all sure that
they would. The whole idea had been to place the bell on

the summit to gain the blessing of the gods for their union.

But, somehow, it had not happened. So nearly, but not quite. And Kami wasn't at all sure what that meant.

And what the implications would be for the future.

Kami never rang the bell. Chastened, he walked slowly back through the village where he found Kurt looking for him.

'Come with me,' Kurt told him. 'I've got something I want you to hear.'

Kami instantly feared the worst, that some sort of confrontation was in the offing as he was taken to the Westerners' mess tent.

As it happened he was offered a cup of cocoa and Kurt made an announcement. 'I've got an idea. I'm wondering if we should take Kami back to the States with us.'

The words hung in the air for a beat or two before the table reacted.

'Excellent!' Sasha clapped her hands in delight. 'That's a great idea!'

'What's your thinking, Kurt?' Brennan asked him in a cool tone.

Kurt sipped at his Thermos cup of tea and smiled warmly at Kami.

'He's an important part of the story.'

'Too right he is!' Sasha exclaimed.

'I mean the two of you made it to the top together,' Kurt continued, 'and I reckon it might be kind of neat if the two of you do some publicity together.'

'Uh-huh,' Brennan nodded briskly.

'It'll enrich the story. It's kind of heartwarming don't you think? I can just see the two of you on breakfast TV, telling it how it was up there on the summit ridge. The two of you achieving that ultimate dream!'

'That is genius!' Sasha chimed. 'The papers will love it, the magazines, everyone. It's the whole human dimension of the ascent. How the two of you started off hardly knowing each other and ended up as fellow summiteers and best buddies.'

'Survivors of the storm,' Kurt added with no little satisfaction. 'The voters will *love it*!'

Brennan was staring at his expedition manager with a glassy kind of look. His expression was inscrutable.

'What do you reckon Kami?' Kurt fired at him.

Kami studied his hands and wondered if he was hearing right.

Travel to the USA? Go on television? Talk to rooms full of people? It was a mind-blowing idea, specially coming so quickly after the news about the marriage pact.

He knew this was an exceptional offer and he did not

272

doubt for a moment that it was genuine. Kami had met other Sherpas who had been invited to the West by their trekking and climbing clients.

Their lives enriched. Their worlds expanded.

Then he thought of something;

'I have no passport,' he told them.

'That's no problem,' Kurt dismissed this with a casual wave of his hand. 'I have people who can fix that. Book you a flight and get you out to the States.'

Kami felt his heart racing with the possibilities, this was truly a once in a lifetime thing.

Could he push his luck? Ask them if he could bring Shreeya too? For a sudden blinding instant he saw a whole universe of new worlds opening up for them both.

Then he locked eyes with Brennan for that split second. And he saw that look and it crushed all hope dead. It was the look he had come to know all too well; the warning flash that told him not to overstep the mark, to move back behind the walls they had erected ... around the lie.

Kami hung his head. Shut his mouth and swallowed the words he had been about to utter.

'Don't you think it might get a bit ... complicated?' Brennan ventured. 'I mean there's the question of a visas and immigration. It might not be as easy as you think to get him in. Homeland security and all that.'

'Get out of here!' Sasha gave him a withering look. 'You can sort that in the blink of an eye.'

'I thought you'd be delighted with the idea,' Kurt said in a hurt tone. 'You've always fought for the ethnic vote. People will love the fact that this Sherpa guy became your friend.'

'It's OK,' Kami got to his feet as he understood what he had to do. 'I cannot go anyway.'

'Can't go?' Sasha asked him. 'Why ever not?'

'My family need me here,' he told them. 'There are fields to be ploughed. Potatoes to be harvested. They cannot do without me.'

Kurt and Sasha began to protest but Kami stood and left the table.

He quit the lodge and ran down the alley towards the river. A few moments later he heard footsteps behind him, Sasha's voice calling for him to stop.

'That was weird,' Sasha said. 'It was, like, you were all up for it and your eyes were shining and then, then you looked at Alex and that light in your eyes went off. It just died. And I saw it.'

'That's not it,' Kami told her urgently. 'I remembered my duties, that's all.'

Sasha put her hand on Kami's shoulder, spun him gently

so he was forced to look her in the face, into those cool green eyes.

'What's *happening*, Kami? What's happening between you and Alex?'

'Nothing.' Kami tried to break away but she continued to hold his shoulder and he could not escape her gaze.

'There's this terrible atmosphere building up between the two of you. You can cut it with a knife, Kami. Even Kurt's starting to pick up on it.'

'Everything is fine.'

Sasha fixed him with her most sceptical look.

'I don't think so. Please tell me about it, Kami, you can trust me as a friend.'

That's exactly what Brennan told me she would say, Kami thought.

'It's not so easy,' he mumbled. 'Please, I have to go back to the others, I have work to do for Tenzing.'

Sasha's expression changed as a new thought suddenly hit her; a new realisation.

'Something happened up there on the mountain didn't it?'

Kami hurried away, desperate to escape the encounter. Sasha ran after him.

'Kami, tell me. *Please.*'

Kami shook his head and walked away into the village.

○

From that point on, during the final two days of the walk out to Lukla, Kami lived with his nerves on a hair trigger of nervous anticipation.

They made it down to Namche, then continued down the precipitous valley side. Then came the suspension bridge crossings and a night at Dughla before the final triumphant haul up to Lukla, where the expedition pulled into the garden of the Khumbu lodge exactly eight weeks and six days after it had left.

'Just to let you know, the boss will be giving out the bonuses at the party tomorrow night,' Tenzing told the Sherpa team with some relish.

That news caused a ripple of excitement amongst Lopsang and the others but Kami felt nothing. He had already paid the debt he needed to pay and all he wanted to do was to get out of that place and return to his village and Shreeya.

But there was still work to do and he could not shirk his responsibilities to Tenzing.

A determined snowfall began early the next day, feathery flakes settling contentedly on wooden shingle roofs and drifting into the alleyways of Lukla. There were no flights out of the airstrip. The little town felt hushed and closed down.

Every time Sasha came within sight he tried to make himself scarce but the town was a small one and he couldn't hide forever. As it was, she tracked him down in the equipment store and asked to speak; 'I got an email from my editor this morning,' she told him. 'Some famous climber contacted him to say he thought the summit picture of Alex was a fake. He said the rock in the background matched a place lower down the ridge.'

Kami said nothing. This was it. The moment he had feared above all.

'Is that true, Kami? Tell me.'

Kami watched clouds racing around the jagged profiles of nearby peaks. He had the sense that he was going into freefall, that the ground would surely swallow him up for this unforgiveable breach of confidence.

Then something snapped inside. He couldn't hold it any more.

'We never reached the top,' Kami told her in a rush. 'You are right. The summit photo was a lie.'

Sasha's face went white as she thought this through.

'Oh my god.'

'Yes. I am so sorry for deceiving everyone.'

Sasha took Kami's hand and he held her tight. There was

a touching connection between them in that moment, as if she was trying to convey to him that she meant him no harm.

'Kami. This is really important. Was it your idea to do that? To fake the picture?'

The truth. It had to be truth from now on.

'No,' he told her softly. 'It was not my idea.'

And with that he walked away.

The hours were ticking away. The party getting closer and closer.

Part of Kami's problem was that he couldn't second guess what Sasha would do; would she confront Brennan with what he had told her? Or would she just write a scathing article to send back to the States?

He waited for the explosion. But somehow it didn't come. Then he learned that Alex and Kurt had gone to the lodge to fix up the party which would celebrate the end of the expedition and it gave him some breathing space.

The afternoon dragged slowly, cleaning ropes, washing sleeping bags in special cleaning solution, eyes smarting from the fumes. Then the hour came and it was time. Kami tried to make some last minute excuses but he was told – with a firm smile – to shut up by Tenzing and to come along with the rest of them.

Inside the lodge, the dining hall had been converted into a makeshift ballroom. Prayer flags had been strung up like bunting. A trestle table was groaning under the weight of the beer bottles that covered it. Lady Gaga was pumping out of the speakers, the Khumbu region's only DJ doing his stuff.

Someone had managed to find some disco lights, pulsing quasars of green, red and blue that sucked up so much power they threatened to blow the town generator to smithereens. A gang of the expeditioners were already dancing, others making a bee-line for the table filled with sandwiches and samosas.

Kami was looking out for Sasha when he felt a strong slap between his shoulder blades. It was Alex Brennan; 'Take a beer,' the boss told him, handing him a can.

'OK.' Kami took a long drink. All he was thinking was 'Does he know? Has Sasha confronted him?'

'You seem depressed, Kami.'

'No, sir. Just ready to be going home.'

'Nothing else that you want to talk about?'

'I'm OK, sir. Just wanting to get back to my family.'

Brennan nodded. 'You won't forget our agreement will you, Kami?'

Kami drank deeply on the beer, not knowing what on earth he could say. So he just nodded.

'Good. And if there's anything more I can ever do for you or your family … you can always count on me as a friend.'

'Thank you, sir.'

'Have a great party, Kami. I'll see you later.'

Brennan moved away and Kami finished off another beer. His head started to pound with the effects of the music and the alcohol. He began to feel nauseous.

'Come and get some food,' Lopsang called him.

Kami shook his head and instead went to seek out Sasha. He found her sitting in the corner of the ballroom, looking pensive and evidently not in a party mood.

'You haven't told him,' Kami began.

'Not yet,' Sasha said, 'but that doesn't mean that nothing's happening.'

'I should not have said what I said. Please forget about it, I beg you.'

'Kami. It's too late to stop this now.'

Kami felt tears prick at the back of his eyes.

'You did good, Kami,' Sasha continued soothingly. 'If he can lie about what happened up there, then who knows what he might lie about in the future. We can't let him get away with it. There's too much at stake.'

At that moment, Tenzing came up.

'There's someone here to see you.' The Sirdar told Kami.

Suddenly the crowd parted and Kami saw a figure entering through the doorway. It was Jamling; weakened and looking fragile after his hospital ordeal, but with that mischievous glint firmly back in his eyes. The veteran Sherpa had travelled back from Kathmandu specially to congratulate Kami on his summit success.

Kami stood there, fixed rigidly to the spot, a growing sense of horror welling up inside him as Jamling picked up a walking stick and slowly shuffled across the room towards him. The guests fell silent as they watched, sensing that they were about to witness raw emotion.

It was the shining excitement in Jamling's eyes that finally did it. The tears of joy that were already beginning to well up. The look of unconditional pride that said, 'You made it.'

But he hadn't made it.

Kami felt he was about to faint. He could feel Brennan's nervous eyes boring into him, watching intently to see how he would handle himself. He caught Sasha's gaze; her look was intense, she knew what was wrong, sensed how close to panic he was.

Kami took a step back. His head was swimming with shame and he could take it no more. He could not allow himself Jamling's embrace.

He caught the flash of confusion – of hurt – in Jamling's eyes as he turned … and ran.

O

Kami burst out of the lodge and hit the path. Hard sleet drummed hard against his face. The rocky trail was cloaked with snow and he was in it up to his calves as he raced up the track.

Lightning split the night; a rolling crescendo of thunder just a heartbeat behind.

In that strobing beat of light he could see the blue gleam of soaring snowfields, thousands of feet above the village. Then the night reclaimed them as he pulled the shrine bell out of his jacket pocket.

'Kami!' A faint cry. Someone had followed him out of the lodge. Was it Brennan? Or someone else? Kami couldn't tell.

He hurried through the town, racing by houses which were shuttered down for the night. A horse reared as he ran by, he slipped on ice then regained his feet as he passed out of Lukla and onto the mountain trail.

Onwards. Steeper now. Gasping for breath but never slowing.

He passed a shepherd's hut, the air thick with the smell of wood smoke. Two jet black dogs came snarling out of the shadows. Wet fur bristling. Glowing embers for eyes. They snapped at his ankles. Still he kept running, the shrine bell in his hand, as cries continued somewhere behind him. A woman's voice was amongst them; Sasha? Again, too distant to be sure.

He climbed and climbed. Faster than he thought possible, spurred by some pulse inside him. Far below he could hear the rush of a mighty river, above him the frozen sleet was settling thickly, loading the slopes with millions of tons of unstable snow.

The path went right. Kami went left. Out onto the snow-field. Right beneath the steepest face.

He was only wearing trainers but he didn't care. He slipped and slid and clawed his way up the snow slope, ripping his nails but not registering the pain.

Behind him came lights. Hunting him down.

Breathing in snatches. Lungs on fire. The mountain a vast monolith above him, shrouded in night clouds and dark as hell. Somewhere up there were avalanche slopes, silent, brooding, ready to wreak havoc. Million-ton bullets waiting to be chambered in nature's game of Russian roulette. At the base was the rocky cave that the other Sherpas had told him about. A hard place of worship. A hidden shrine.

He could see the dark cave – and the light flickering inside.

He continued up the slope, got to the shrine. Indra's shrine – the god of thunder and war. The flame was comforting. A candle of hope in this night of turbulence and electric air. A fitting night for this fiery god.

Thunder rolled above. Brittle snaps of noise which sent balls of lightning spitting far across the valley.

He brought out the shrine bell. Clutched it like a talisman to his breast as he chanted the words of a timeless prayer. A plate of flowers was there. The petals shrivelled but perhaps the gods would not care. He scattered them around the image of Indra, while cries of 'Kami' rang shrill across the snowfield.

Footsteps were approaching. Faster. Faster.

'Gods will you forgive me?' Kami muttered.

He rang the bell, the sound clear and light against the thunderous roar of the storm. Shreeya was so far away but in this moment of delusion he imagined she might hear that noise and be heartened by it.

'Kami!' Dark shapes were out there, picking a precarious way across to the shrine.

'Leave me alone!' he yelled. But his scream was swallowed up with a further mighty clap of thunder and through the driving snow he could see a vast shape racing down from the threatening slope.

Avalanche. He stepped out of the shrine and stood there, watching in awe as the night became a solid, threatening force.

The roar of the airborne snow merged with the rolling thunder of the tempest until it was impossible to tell which part of the wall of sound was avalanche and which was storm. It sounded like the whole mountain had split in two.

'Run! RUN!' Brennan's scream was raw.

Kami turned. He knew it was pointless to run further.

And suddenly he understood; he had asked the gods for forgiveness and this was their answer.

It was all so clear. And death was so close.

Kami raised his arms. If this was his fate then he wanted to face it without fear. Then a dark shape flew across the ice slope towards him, half running, half falling. It was Sasha and the last thing Kami remembered feeling was her body wrapping around him, protecting him, cradling his head and bracing herself for the impact as the mighty wall of snow tumbled down the slope towards them.

Then they were swept away, glissading, the night air filling with powdered ice as Kami felt the darkness engulf him.

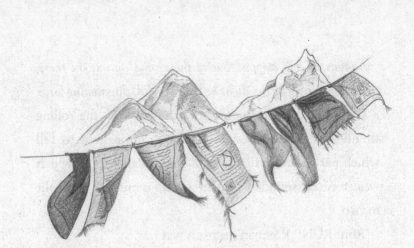

CHAPTER 12

The sun was low in the sky. The shutters of Kami's little bedroom were casting long shadows across the room. I looked at my watch. It was almost 5 p.m. Kami had talked through the whole day and he was now so wiped out he could barely keep his eyes open.

I was also exhausted but I felt no need of a rest; in fact I would have listened to Kami for days on end if he could have continued. The whole story had been shocking, not least because of the totally unflattering portrait it painted of Alex Brennan, a man I had admired on the occasions I had seen him interviewed on TV.

Above all, there was a vitality to Kami's telling of the tale, an urgency, a total lack of self-pity that was quite amazing.

'Don't cry,' he had told me several times during the story. 'There is no time for crying.'

Dawa entered the room. 'Better you let him sleep now,' he said. He had looked after us kindly during the long hours, bringing us lentils and rice and tea.

I gently unfolded my fingers from Kami's hand, and picked up the tray of empty dishes and tea cups. I took them to Dawa's little hut and washed them clean before walking out onto the patio. The afternoon had a mellow feel to it and I stretched my arms above my head to ease some stiffness.

Then I remembered the shadow I had seen at the bottom of the cliff, the half-seen figure that had spooked me when I had first arrived. That sensation of being watched. The odd conviction that someone, or something was there – silent, ever vigilant.

I re-entered the bungalow, 'Dawa!' I called to him urgently, 'Kami never told me about the carer. Can you ... ?'

But Dawa shook his head firmly.

'I have told you that I am not permitted to speak of this,' he said politely. And he closed the door.

I was uncertain about what to do. Should I try and kill my curiosity? I had seen Kami, after all, and heard his whole story. Wasn't that enough?

But *was it* the whole story? I still wasn't sure.

So I wandered to the forest edge and stared towards the cliff face which was hidden there. Through small gaps in the trees I could see the darker texture of rock. High above the trees I could see the upper reaches of the outcrop – two or three hundred metres high.

I noticed a track, not much more than a faint line of compressed earth. I followed it, a meandering trail of some thirty metres which stopped abruptly at the rock face.

Standing at the foot of the cliff I craned my neck backwards and gazed vertically up towards the high stony lip. Scudding gangs of clouds were streaming past and the cliff seemed to be tottering with them. It was seriously steep, I realised, and not something I would want to try and climb without a rope and a partner.

But then I saw the slick shine of bamboo. A series of rickety ladders had been built up the face, and I guessed they were probably the work of honey hunters. I counted six or seven leading up and the hint of some dark cavity set into the rock at the high point.

I crossed to the first of the ladders and gave it a shake. It felt rugged enough but the thought of committing my life to those flimsy things was seriously scary. I wasted a bit of time hunting around the base of the cliff for some easier trail upwards but there was none so I steeled myself for the climb.

I stepped onto the ladder. The rungs were brittle, fractured with age; with every nervous move upwards I felt my weight could shatter them to bits. A creeping fungus had attacked the bamboo; the wood was mottled with powdery black mould and my hands quickly became stained with the dark spores.

Two more ladders gained me another twenty metres or so of height and spat me out, panting hard, on a section of broken-up ground where scrambling was possible.

I found a dry patch of rock where I could rest my legs and I was pleased to see how much height I had gained. Far below, the bungalow seemed no bigger than a doll's house. It looked like the slightest flash flood could sweep the whole place away in the blink of an eye.

I traversed across the face and came to the next steep section; it was back to the ladders.

These final sections of bamboo felt even more dodgy than the ones lower down. There were places where the whole thing seemed to be held in place by little more than tendrils of moss and caterpillar spit. It swayed and creaked and groaned under my weight, and I could easily imagine myself crashing down to the valley floor hundreds of feet below in a blizzard of ripped-out rocks and bits of bamboo.

A bee came to investigate. It buzzed around my head for a few seconds and then landed on one of the rungs to check me out, its furry orange body pumping as it rested.

Then another arrived. I swatted it away, but my movement attracted several more of the insects and I got a sudden spasm of fear.

Suddenly across the cliff face, just a few metres away, I saw the hive, a massive honeycomb completely covered with tens of thousands of the bees.

As I watched in horrified fascination the bees somehow simultaneously changed their body positions, causing a shift of colour from indigo-black to a warning flash of orange-red and then back again. The thing looked like a vast evil eye and I knew that there was nowhere I could run to.

The buzzing of the hive seemed to rise a few notches, become angrier.

Suddenly a voice came from above. A rich American voice.

'Don't worry about the bees. They won't touch you this late in the day. Come on up.'

I saw a long haired figure silhouetted against the juddering clouds. Then it retreated back into the rock.

As I reached the final rung of the ladder I realised I was looking into the dark interior of a cave. The final move up off the ladder was a tricky one and I made a clumsy job of it, but a strong hand shot out of the gloom and I clasped it gratefully as I lumbered up over the lip and found myself on a narrow rocky balcony.

I looked into the cave. And there, partly obscured in the shadows, was Alex Brennan.

'Who were you expecting?' he asked with a smile. 'Marlon Brando?'

He shifted his position and gestured for me to enter the cave. As my eyes adjusted to the low light I could see the shelter was the size of a small room. The floor was dry and covered with Indian-style rugs. A few meagre possessions were heaped in the corner, a sleeping bag, a metal box, some pots and pans.

Brennan was bare footed, dressed in a faded T-shirt and a tatty pair of jeans. He was not much changed from Kami's description of him, the blonde locks a little longer and more matted perhaps, the athletic tone of his body softened and not so sharp.

My mind was in catch-up mode, in a kind of shock. I had figured that Kami's mysterious carer would be a local person, a holy man perhaps or maybe a member of his family. Not for a moment had I thought that it would be the great Alex Brennan himself ...

'Kami's a special person, don't you think?' he said.

I could only nod my agreement.

'You want some tea?'

He brought out a brightly-coloured Thermos flask from beneath a blanket. I nodded my thanks and he poured the yellow fluid into a chipped china bowl.

'Dawa makes it,' he said as he offered me the cup, 'it's really not so bad when you get used to it.'

I sipped at the lukewarm tea.

'You were watching me these last days,' I said.

'Just checking you out. Plus I had to put you through a forty-eight-hour quarantine to make sure you weren't carrying some bug.'

Stupidly, I hadn't thought of that. But it did make perfect sense. Kami was hardly in a position to fight off infection and even a dose of flu could kill him.

'I guess he told you everything?' he continued.

'As far as the avalanche.'

'Ah. And did he tell you Sasha died?'

'No.' I digested this news, feeling real sorrow. Kami had painted an affectionate picture of the American journalist even if their friendship hadn't always been straightforward.

'I thought he probably wouldn't go that far,' Brennan went on carefully, 'that's where the story gets real hard for him.

She was trying to protect him. When we dug them out of the snow she was curled around his body, cradling his head, shielding him from the ice blocks.'

Brennan sipped his tea.

'She gave her life for him,' he said simply, 'that was an outstanding thing to do.'

Somewhere outside the cave I could hear birds – black ravens – play-fighting up and down the cliffs.

'Did she post a final article before she died?' I asked.

'Oh sure. I found a draft of it in her tent after the avalanche. Kami had told her everything and she'd already emailed it back to New York. That was her job after all.'

'Did it get published? I don't remember seeing anything about it.'

'No. It never made it into print. It didn't need to. Word had already got out all over Washington. I had my enemies, people who wanted to bring me down. Sometimes they prefer to sit on something like that to neutralise you. It's more powerful that way, once they had that ammunition I was finished as a politician.'

'But why this?' I gestured to the Spartan interior of the cave. 'Are you a holy man now?'

Brennan kind of laughed.

'Let's just say I had a bit of a re-think on my life,' he said.

'Threw away all the things I didn't need and took a different path.'

'A religious one.'

'Some might think that,' he said. 'I do a lot of meditation. A lot of thinking. But really I'm just here to do the right thing for Kami. For as long as I can.'

'And the secrecy? Why did you come here of all places?'

Brennan shook his head. 'That was Kami. He picked this place himself. I think he felt he had caused too much upset, too much grief to those he loved. He thought it was easier for everyone if he just disappeared.'

'He's become something of a legend.'

'He's earned that,' Brennan laughed. 'That's the least he deserves.'

I drank more of the tea.

'Do you ever go home? I mean back to the States?'

'No. I sold everything. Cut away from all the people I cared for and who cared for me.'

'That must have been tough.'

'I'm not saying it's easy,' he agreed, 'being nobody is a whole lot harder than being somebody, believe me.'

Brennan manoeuvred himself to the mouth of the cave and beckoned me over to his side so we could look out over the valley.

'I want to show you something … Look, over there.'

I followed his oustretched arm and I suddenly noticed something really quite amazing. The encroaching night had plunged the valley into near darkness and the far wall was a distant rampart of green-black rock.

But there was something else.

There, resting just a *fraction* higher than the barrier of deep shadow, I could see the tiny triangle of a single sunlit peak. It was far away – very far in fact, collecting the dying rays of the sun which was setting somewhere out of view. The impression was of a golden pinpoint of light, an illuminated pyramid resting magically on a dark wall. It was a stunning visual effect.

'Now you know why I chose this place,' Brennan said softly. 'I get to see my nemesis every evening.'

'Your nemesis?'

Then I felt stupid. Of *course* it was Everest, what else could it possibly be? Only the ultimate summit could jut so far towards the heavens as to be visible from this distance.

I drank in the splendour of the scene, concentrating hard, wanting to lock the moment away in my memory for ever it was so mesmerising.

'I did see a holy man for a while,' he said quietly. 'Do you know what he told me?'

'What?'

'He said that the day I would be reborn, the day I would be free, would be the day I could look on that vision and not feel even the slightest degree of pain or regret.'

I could see the sunlight was dying on the summit.

'Are you getting close?'

Brennan sighed. 'I'm not there yet,' he said, 'but one day … maybe.'

He stared off to the distance as the conversation petered out and seemed not to share the embarrassment I felt at the silence. It was disturbing to gaze at him in those moments; like looking at the calm surface of a reservoir when you know there is a sunken village drowned in its depths, or gazing at a vast field of innocent grass in some quiet rural place when you know there are musketballs and flintlocks buried deep in the mulch from some ancient bloody battle.

Then Brennan broke the spell, just at the same instant that the light on Everest's summit finally died away.

'You really have to go,' he told me urgently, 'you don't want to be doing those ladders in the dark.'

He was right. The prospect was terrifying. I had already stayed too long but one last question was pressing me;

'How long do you think you will live here?' I asked him.

Brennan thought about it. 'One day maybe one of those

ladders will break,' he said with a wry smile, 'that or the bees will get me. So long, my friend, go well.'

With that he melted back into the shadows of the cave.

I made it down the ladders with just enough light to guide me and slept soundly in my tent that night. In the morning Dawa prepared me fried eggs and chapattis and later we went into Kami's room so I could say goodbye.

'Give my love to Shreeya,' he murmured. He seemed weak after the efforts of the previous day, slipping in and out of a state of sleep but still able to give me that beatific smile.

'He needs a few days of absolute rest,' Dawa told me, 'then he will be fine again.'

I trusted his judgement. Kami was well cared for. I kissed him on the forehead by way of parting.

I packed away my tent and Dawa gripped my hand hard. A military handshake from an old soldier.

'It has been a pleasure to have you here,' he said sincerely. 'Thank you.'

He helped me to put on my pack and I set off down the trail. On the forest edge, I took one last look back at the bungalow – that curious place which was at the same time a sanctuary, a hospital and a prison for Kami.

Then my eyes tipped skywards, to the dark smudge high on the cliff.

Brennan's final words re-ran in my mind and I prayed for Kami's sake that they would not be true.

O

Three days later I got back to Shreeya's village. It had been a tough trek; the journey had been a wet one with no porter to help with the load. Non-stop rainstorms had turned the track into a muddy slipway and I was relieved to make it to the safety and warmth of the village that had become my temporary home.

I went straight to Shreeya's house and gave her the news about Kami. Naturally she was overjoyed to hear that Kami was alive, but the tragic circumstance of his paralysis was something she had never contemplated and I could see it was as huge a shock to her as it had been to me.

'Can he be cured?' she asked, her face white. 'Will he ever walk again?'

I had to tell her no.

Shreeya devoured every detail of my tale then more questions spilled out: who paid for Kami's keep? What food did he eat? Could he breathe all right?

Then the question that moved me the most:

Could he laugh as well as talk?

'Yes,' I told her, 'he can laugh like you or me. His mind is still positive. And he talks of you above all else.'

This last statement gave her great comfort and she shed a few small tears. Her aunt, who had sat through all of this saying nothing, now took up her normal stance which was to whine at Shreeya. I couldn't decipher every aspect of what she was saying but it was clear she hated even the slightest mention of Kami's name in her house.

The scolding went on, Shreeya trying to ignore it. I was longing for sleep. The long trek back to the village had exhausted me and I knew that the next few days would also involve some hard travelling to get back to Kathmandu. But the increasingly tense mood of the evening was putting me on edge, and I knew instinctively that Shreeya and her aunt were gearing up for a fight.

As I went to my room I heard distant thunder rumbling across the valley. Through the splits in the wooden shutter I could see intense flashes of lightning. The sour tone of the conversation in the kitchen had degenerated into a bitter row, interspersed with tears and recriminations.

I heard Shreeya run to her room. A door slammed. Then there were footsteps and a painful sounding thud as the aunt dragged Shreeya from her bed with a series of curses.

I had grown used to these arguments, sometimes continuing late into the night, but the intensity of this fight seemed somehow on a different scale. Normally it was only the aunt's voice I could hear, nagging at Shreeya, browbeating her as her niece sat soaking it up.

But tonight Shreeya was giving as good as she got. And that wasn't going down well at all. Nothing infuriated the aunt more than Shreeya answering her back, and tonight she was really going for it. The two of them got more and more shrill, rising in intensity as the aunt's voice stepped up to become a sort of continuous irritating whine.

As the storm hit its peak, the argument went nuclear and I knew I could no longer stay out of it. A beating was in progress in the kitchen and Shreeya's cries were blood curdling. Pots and pans were flying. I heard the heavy iron cauldron hit the floor.

I hurriedly pulled on some trousers and a T-shirt and ran down the stairs to the kitchen.

The scene was truly awful, Shreeya with her hands clutched against her head, bent into a submissive posture as the aunt slapped and scratched and ripped out clumps of her hair. At the same moment the storm hit its peak, the claps of thunder coming every few seconds, great waves of hail beating like bullet strikes against the slate roof just inches above my head.

'Please! You must stop!' I tried to pull the aunt away

from behind but she stood her ground, jabbing me with a sharp elbow in the guts and yelling every Nepali curse under the sun. I seized her again and all three of us fell in a jumble into the corner of the room, smashing against the table and collapsing it immediately.

The paraffin lamp went flying, the glass windshade shattering on the floor as flaming paraffin spread liquid fire over the compacted earth. The aunt was so hysterical she seemed hardly to notice, the beating continuing as Shreeya screamed at me to put out the flames.

I grabbed a blanket, threw it on the floor and smothered the heart of the fire. Then I grabbed another and beat at the edges until the flames were extinguished. The room filled with black smoke, occasional dazzling strobes of lightning punching through the gaps in the shutters as the storm still raged.

The awful stench of paraffin and burnt yak hair filled the room.

The aunt backed off as smoke filled her lungs. She threw open a window and leaned out in the search for clean air. I gave Shreeya my hand and helped her up. She stood there, white-faced and in shock, staring directly into the beam of my head torch like it had hypnotised her.

Ugly bruises were already flowering on her neck.

'You are not my family,' she told the aunt. The woman did not reply.

Shreeya went to her room once again and this time the aunt did not follow. I cleared up some of the mess in the kitchen while the old woman stared out of the window at the fading storm.

I left her there, still gazing with disturbing intensity into the night, went to my room and folded the sleeping bag around me. Gradually, the storm burned itself out, thunder diminishing until it was the merest hint of turbulence somewhere to the south.

The house was quiet but I was sure nobody was sleeping.

The first grey whisper of dawn brought a quiet knocking at my door. Shreeya entered, already dressed, her face filled with light despite the dark bruises that the beating had given her.

'I am going to go to him,' she said simply. 'You have to tell me how … '

Once the words had been uttered I saw the beauty of her decision and the breathtaking courage that had enabled it to happen. Shreeya was right to escape from the poisonous grip of her aunt. The woman was a parasite intent on destroying her spirit. Also Shreeya was clearly still emotionally tied to Kami and there was nothing to stop them being together. Above all, Shreeya's presence would give Kami new hope, help him to move on from the long shadow of Brennan's expedition.

Everything about it was right.

'I will take you,' I offered. I could re-arrange my flight, find a new air ticket home if necessary. Anything to help.

'Thank you, but no,' she replied instantly. 'I want to go alone.'

I explained just what an undertaking the journey was. The long climb into the hidden valley. The leeches. The lonely nights in the forest.

But she shrugged these things off with a smile and I saw in her eyes a shadow of that extraordinary self-conviction that had enabled her to save those snow leopards all those years before.

I brought out the map and explained to Shreeya the journey I had made. I gave her a day-by-day account of the trek into that wild valley, mentioning some of the landmarks along the way.

'It is more than seventy kilometres,' I reminded her.

'It could be one thousand and I still wouldn't care.'

More questions followed, far more practical than those of the night before. Where could she find water? Was there food for sale in that final village? Did I meet kind people along the trail? Were there any dangerous rivers to cross?

Suddenly we heard the sound of the aunt, stirring in her room.

'I have to move quickly,' Shreeya said.

'What are you going to take with you?' I asked her.

'Just this.' Shreeya showed me a little wrapped up bundle of clothes.

Seeing that sad little collection of possessions I shook my belongings out of my rucksack and gave it to her. Then I thought further and added my tent, two water bottles, a rain jacket and a handful of local currency. She accepted these gifts with simple grace, placing her few possessions into the pack and adding some biscuits and dried fruit.

We crept down the stairs, moving carefully through the animals' night quarters where the chickens were just clucking out of their sleep.

Shreeya eased the creaky old wooden door open and we hurried through the village, past the sealed-up doorways, past the curled-up dogs – too sleepy to bark an alarm. Down to the village well we ran, the dawn air filled with intense scents of damp earth and animal dung. I filled the two bottles with clear, cool water and placed them in the side pockets of the pack.

'Do you want me to show you how to put up the tent?' I asked her.

Shreeya glanced nervously back at the village where her aunt could even now be discovering her empty bed.

'There is no time. I have to hurry.'

I walked with her to the place where the fields began. Then it was time to part. We stood for a few moments, neither of us sure what to say or how to conduct ourselves. Then I embraced her and she hugged me back warmly for a moment or two.

Then she was searching for something in her bag.

'I want you to take this,' she said.

And she handed me the shrine bell, a gesture that touched me so deeply that I truly had no idea how to respond.

'Kami would want you to have it,' she said. 'For everything that you have done for us. And who knows, maybe one day you will be able to give it to someone who can take it up there, to the home of the gods where it belongs?'

And with those startling words she took a couple of paces backwards, then turned and began her journey. I watched her for a while as she trekked confidently along the path, her small figure traversing along the valley side and then turning the corner so that she could no longer be seen.

An unstoppable wave of tiredness swept over me at that moment, the virtually sleepless night catching up with me. I yawned deeply and thought about heading back to the aunt's house to rest but then decided I couldn't face the inquisition which would inevitably follow.

Besides, Shreeya's gift was now in my hands and I needed to think about things, so I trekked up one of the narrow pathways which flanked the village, heading for the pretty little meadow which looked out across the whole of the Himalayan range.

The place that had been a secret refuge for Kami and Shreeya.

The rains had finally stopped and the ground was drying out fast. When I reached the glade I found the place was carpeted with so many wild flowers I could hardly take a step without crushing one. Thistledown was floating lazily upwards and the sky was alive with swifts.

I found a resting place on an old log and sat there with the shrine bell cradled in my hands. I looked at it closely, noting the age-polished teak of the handle, the delicate engravings which chased about the bronze.

There was plenty of cloud about, the normal morning mists and fogs. But gradually it began to shift as the sun got the upper hand.

A fleeting peephole opened up. A hazy summit revealed, far higher and greater than seemed possible.

Everest again. On show. Peerless and proud. I wondered if,

in that moment, I was the only person in the world to be looking at that home of legends, birthplace of great glaciers, of mighty meltwater rivers.

And, for some, place of broken dreams.

As I thought about it, I realised that this was the third time I had seen the peak. The first time had been from the aircraft window at the beginning of my journey, an encounter of absolute innocence, the peak had meant nothing more to me than a photo opportunity at that point – spectacular though it had been. The second had been from the vantage point of Alex Brennan's cave, a moment loaded with the emotion of what I had learned about Kami's journey – and filled, in a real sense, with his pain.

How much darker had the mountain seemed on that second view; seen through the magnifying lens of the tragedy that had befallen Kami. A place of dangerous obsession, a testing ground in which even the strongest of men were found wanting.

A changer of lives. And not always for the good.

And now? The third time to gaze on that summit. The most dangerous time of all. Because now, much to my surprise, the mountain was speaking to me directly. A line of communication had somehow been opened, lighting a fire inside that I could never have imagined. My heart began to race. I felt my breathing quicken. I turned the shrine bell over and over, then clutched it tight in my hands, wanting to keep the metal warm as I dared to imagine ...

And I felt my blood run as cold as ice.

Because the mountain was calling ...

Calling ...

And I did not know if I had the power to resist.

END OF BOOK ONE

WITH THANKS TO ...

Writing a book is rather similar to climbing Everest. A long hard slog filled with unexpected dramas, cruel twists of fate and the constant fear of failure. And you never see the summit right until the end!

But it's worth it when you hold the finished book in your hand.

With this first book in the Everest Files series I have been fortunate to have the support of some remarkable people so let's start from the beginning. First off, my heart-felt thanks to Brian Blessed; without his passion and love of Everest my own summit experience would never have happened. Next came the germ of the 'Everest Files' story, and a fruitful ideas session with Fee Dickinson at a rather good pizza house in Tring.

Fast forward a few years; writing draft after draft with the help and inspiration of Chris Bradley, Sim Canetty-Clarke, Nicholas Crane and Steve Varden. My super literary agent, Alice Williams, then entered the frame with tenacious commitment and charm.

Among my Oxford friends Sarah Darby and Sorrel Pitts have never wavered in their belief that the book should be published. In their precious spare time they have given valuable advice and Sarah kindly created the chapter heading illustrations that have added considerable charm to the book. That legendary traveller and writer Hilary Bradt was also a source of encouragement and hope in the dark times when we really struggled to find a good home for this book.

Thanks also to the others that have helped the concept grow: Jon Stefani and Seni Glaister for cool mountain inspiration; Nigel Barlow and Angie Kaye for a good glass of wine; Dave Cousins and his wife Jane for a pair of Mexican underpants (don't ask); Asif Moghal and Geraldine Colclough for aiming high; Gill Lewis for a whole load of laughs and Ruth Eastham for two cups of tea.

Above all I am blessed with the love and support of my family so a big kiss and hug to; Anna, Tom, Ali, Greg, Daniel, Ariadna and my mother Sheila. I absolutely could not have done this without you.

Finally, I reached the summit and found a mountain-crazy publishing team that really believe in the book, and the series it has now created. So my sincere thanks to Jon Barton, Nathan Ryder, and the award-winning team at Vertebrate Publishing.

Hold on tight, guys. It's going to be a wild ride!

ABOUT THE AUTHOR

Matt Dickinson is an award-winning writer and filmmaker with a passion for climbing and adventure. During his filmmaking career he has worked as a director/cameraman for National Geographic television, the Discovery channel, the BBC and Channel 4. His film projects have taken him to Antarctica, Africa and the Himalaya, often in the company of the world's leading climbers and expeditioners. His most notable film success was *Summit Fever*, in which he reached the summit of Everest via the treacherous North Face. His book *The Death Zone* tells the true story of that ascent and has become a bestseller in many different countries.

Matt is currently writer in residence for the Laurus Trust and patron of reading at Fortismere School, and he continues to climb and explore. In January 2013 he summited Mount Aconcagua, which, at 6,965 metres, is the highest peak in the world outside the Himalaya. In 2016, and again in 2017, he was back on Everest as a writer in residence, and he is planning an ascent of Denali in Alaska, one of the 'seven summits'.

Matt has written fiction for teenage readers – his debut thriller series Mortal Chaos was well received by critics and readers alike, and he followed this up with the Everest Files, a dramatic and popular trilogy set on the world's highest mountain. *Lie Kill Walk Away* is his latest teen thriller. He has also started writing books for younger readers with his new series following the adventures of the Popcorn-Eating Squirrels. When he's not writing, Matt tours the UK, speaking at schools and colleges and inspiring a new generation of adventurers.

Fascinated by Everest?
Want to know more about the world's highest peak?

The Everest Files website is packed full of fascinating facts and features.

- Find out about Everest, the Himalaya and the effect global warming is having on the area. Geographical facts with study guides for teachers.
- Watch the summit footage taken by the Everest Files author Matt Dickinson after his epic North Face ascent.
- Discover more about the Sherpa people and their way of life.
- See an interview with Jordan Romero, the thirteen-year-old boy who became the youngest person ever to summit Everest.
- Learn more about the Everest Files trilogy, including a video message from author Matt Dickinson.

If you would like an author visit from Matt Dickinson for your school or club, contact details can be found on the website.

www.everestfiles.com